Demon Blood

Bonnie La

Copyright

This book is a work of fiction. Names, characters, places, dialogue and incidents either are the product of the author's imagination or are used fictitiously, and any resemblance to actual events, locales, or persons, living or dead, is entirely coincidental.

Copyright ©2016 by Bonnie Humbarger Lamer

All rights reserved.

No part of this text may be reproduced, transmitted, down-loaded, decompiled, reverse engineered, scanned or distributed in any printed or electronic form without the express written permission of the copyright holder.

ISBN-13: 978-1535455756

ISBN-10: 1535455756

Other Titles by Bonnie Lamer

The Witch Fairy Series:

True of Blood

Blood Prophecy

Blood Lines

Shadow Blood

Blood of Half Gods

Blood of Destiny

Blood of Dragons

Blood of Egypt

Blood of Retribution

Blood of the Exiled

Doppelganger Blood

Blood of Centaurs

Blood of Sirens

Elf Blood

Blood and Spirits

True of Blood: Kallen's Tale

Blood Prophecy: Kallen's Tale

Blood Lines: Kallen's Tale

Shadow Blood: Kallen's Tale

Blood of Half Gods: Kallen's Tale

Blood of Destiny: Kallen's Tale

Blood of Dragon's: Kallen's Tale

Blood of Egypt: Kallen's Tale

Blood of Retribution: Kallen's Tale

Blood of the Exiled: Kallen's Tale

Blood of Centaurs: Kallen's Tale

Blood of Sirens: Kallen's Tale

The Eliana Brennan Series:

Essence of Re

Exposed

Homeland

Sutekh

The Secrets of the Djinn Series:

Marked

Bound

Unchained

I love to hear from fans! Contact me on Facebook at
http://www.facebook.com/pages/Bonnie-Lamer-Author/129829463748061

For my great nieces Kiersten and Karma. I hope you never grow out of being excited to see your Aunt Bonnie.

1 Chapter

"They've come a long way in the last few months," I muse, laying my head on Kallen's shoulder. We are watching my parents walk hand in hand by the shore. They are walking slowly, and carefully, but they are walking. Their atrophied muscles were slow to wake from their years long slumber, and it's good to see them up and about without the physical trainer who comes daily to help them exercise. I offered to try to heal them my way, but they wanted to do it without magic.

"Yes, they have. If their ability to walk returned as readily as your father's appetite, though, they'd be running along the beach by now," Kallen replies with a wink.

I can't help but giggle. As a spirit, Dad missed food the most. Since returning to his body, he has gained a good ten pounds. He was always fit, so no one really notices other than him, but he mentions it a lot. He's eager to be able to exercise more enthusiastically so he can continue to eat what he wants and not worry about it. I try not to roll my eyes when he talks about it. It's ten pounds, for goodness sake.

"Ow!" Kallen suddenly exclaims, rubbing the back of his head.

"Leave the man alone. He hasn't eaten in years," Tabitha scolds.

"I was kidding," Kallen grouses, still rubbing the spot where she smacked him.

Tabitha sets the bowl of fruit she is carrying down on the table. Peering over the sand at my parents, she shakes her head. "I still can't believe it."

"You can't believe we have a Witch and a Cowan living in our realm?" Kegan jests, plucking an apple from the bowl.

"Hey! My mother is a Cowan and she has lived here since before my birth," Alita growls.

Fear suddenly registers in Kegan's eyes wiping away any trace of mirth which once resided there. Since Alita entered the last phase of her pregnancy, her moods have become increasingly difficult to gauge. Generally, though, they run toward being annoyed with everything her husband says and does. At this point, I'm not sure why Kegan hasn't taken a vow of silence until after the baby is born. It would be most beneficial for his health and wellbeing. Tabitha swears Alita's behavior is due to the fact that the end of a pregnancy is extremely uncomfortable and her hormones are completely out of whack. She swears it's not because Alita has finally realized she has married a jerk and is plotting to kill Kegan in his sleep as Kallen likes to insist is the case. Still, Kegan really should have known better than to say something even in teasing regarding a subject Alita is so sensitive about.

"I love your mother," is Kegan's lame response. He knows he's in trouble and there are no words he can think of to get himself out of it.

Tabitha takes a step back toward the house. Kallen takes my hand, ready to pull me out of harm's way. I'm not worried, I'm confident I can put up a magical shield before anything painful happens. To me and Kallen, at least. Kegan is on his own since it was his mouth that got him into this mess. Even I am smart enough not to make teasing comments around Alita right now. About anything. She takes a lot of things personally at the moment.

Magic floods the terrace. "You don't think Cowans should live here, do you?" Alita demands.

Kegan's eyes are wide as they dart from Alita's face to her humongous baby bump. Technically, it is the baby's magic spreading outward from his wife. It is his baby's magic which he needs to fear. I believe he is beginning to worry his baby hates him. Taking a deep breath, Kegan attempts to placate both wife and child. "I think whoever desires to live here in harmony with us should live here. I am delighted that our family is so diverse."

"Liar," Alita hisses. The magic that has thus far been held back is about to be flung forth, which will probably result in Kegan going flying across the sand. Painfully. But instead, we are all shocked when it simply dissolves back to the earth as quickly as it was pulled. A look of wonder crosses Alita's face, which is a nice change from the permascowl she's been wearing lately.
Unfortunately, the look of wonder is immediately followed by a contorted expression of pain.

Kegan is by her side in an instant, all threat of magical punishments forgotten in his haste to be sure she is well. "What is it? What is wrong?"

Since Alita seems beyond words at the moment, it is Tabitha who answers. A wide grin spreads across her face. "From the puddle on the ground, I would say her water just broke."

Kegan turns his now ashen face to the older Fairy. "The baby is coming?" Worry, fear and joy are colliding on his face. It's really rather charming. I elbow Kallen in the ribs when he snickers at his cousin's discomfort.

Alita finds her voice again and she snarks through a contraction, "What, you think it is only raining under my chair? Of course the baby is coming." She attempts to stand, but her center of balance is so off, she has trouble. She holds an expectant hand out to Kegan and he immediately rises and assists her. "Help me upstairs," Alita orders. "I am not having this baby on the terrace." Lord, I love her pregnant. She is such a bossy, take control Fairy right now. I wonder if any of it will stick with her after the baby is born. I hope so. She was too meek before. Studying her closely, I see the pain in her eyes is retreating, so her contraction must be, as well. Good. Unfortunately, there are many more in her near future.

"I will carry you," Kegan insists.

Alita shakes her head and her words are even more insistent. "I can walk. Just help me."

Kegan turns worried eyes to Tabitha for guidance. Tabitha nods. "She is fine to walk. Help her upstairs and

I will be along shortly." The older Fairy turns to Kallen. "Send a message to the midwife while I gather clean linens and the pain potions I made."

"Can I help?" I ask.

Shaking her head, Tabitha says, "No. You better stay out here and keep an eye on your parents. Don't let them tire themselves out too much."

In other words, stay here and out of the way. I get it. And since I've never had any particular desire to be present for the birth of a baby, I'm secretly relieved. Dad showed me a video once during an anatomy lesson when I was homeschooled. So, I know the joy of giving birth is a rather messy, bloody and painful affair. I'm good staying on the beach. Especially since I also know that Alita is in excellent hands with Tabitha and the midwife. "Okay." I watch Alita and Kegan disappear through the door excited for them and their future.

Kallen gives my hand a squeeze. "My cousin is going to be a nervous wreck. If he survives the birth."

"Are you afraid Alita will kill him before it's over?" I ask.

He smirks. "I am almost certain of it."

"What's going on?" Dad asks as he and Mom approach the terrace. Their excursion on the beach has tired them. I can see it in Mom's eyes.

"Alita is in labor," I tell them.

Looking longingly at the door, Dad asks, "Do you think I could be of help?" He missed more than food while he was a spirit. He missed being a doctor, as well.

Mom pats his arm sympathetically. "I'm sure the midwife has everything under control." Dad nods, but the doctor in him is feeling useless at the moment.

"How are you two doing?" I ask to change the subject. "I can't believe how well you're getting around now."

A smile breaks out on Mom's face. "The feel of the ocean on my toes is magical. I tried to convince your father to take a dip with me, but he refused."

I give her a dubious look. "The ocean's a little chilly for swimming right now."

She shrugs, gazing over her shoulder at the water longingly. "Soon then."

Tabitha comes bustling back onto the terrace. "Just got a message from the midwife. She's delivering a Fairy in the village and can't make it." Even without Kallen's mental ability, Fairies are able to send messages with magic. They are simply sent to a notepad Fairies keep in various places instead of a person's mind. Sort of like calling someone and leaving a message. Kallen's method is more efficient as a note can be overlooked for some time. Not in this case, apparently.

Tabitha's eyes move to me and I pale. She can't expect me to deliver a baby. Fortunately, her eyes slide immediately on to Dad. "Jim, we could use a hand if you don't mind." I am not going to be completely left out, though. "Xandra, magical births are a little different than what your father is used to attending. For his safety, you should come along, too. The babe's magic could get out of hand."

Now it's Dad's turn to pale. His eagerness to help has dimmed a little. He recovers quickly, though. "I'm sure I can manage," he says, doing his best to exude confidence.

"Probably, but I'll help anyway." Standing up, I give Kallen a quick hug. "Wish us luck," I whisper in his ear. Kegan might not be the only one in trouble now. The baby has more targets. Hopefully it doesn't remember any of the teasing I did toward Alita earlier in the pregnancy. It was all in good fun. I was never mean. Still, do Fairy babies hold grudges?

"Good luck," Kallen says with a soft chuckle. He must be reading my mind. He gives me a light kiss before leaning back in his chair, getting comfortable.

I eye the chair I just left longingly. With a sigh, I walk to Dad and hold my hand out to him. "Let's teleport upstairs." No sense in wearing him out before he even gets to Alita's room. He doesn't look quite as weary as mom, but he's not as robust as he was this morning, either. He must be thinking the same thing because he doesn't argue. He simply grasps my outstretched hand.

"Good luck, dear," Mom says before Dad and I disappear from the terrace.

A second later in the hall outside Alita and Kegan's room, I ask a now slightly dizzy Dad, "Are you sure you're up for this? It's not too late to say no."

"Are you kidding?" Dad scoffs, straightening his shoulders and reaching for the doorknob. "This is the first time I've felt useful in years. It's about time I earned my keep around here."

I roll my eyes. "No one is keeping score, Dad." He ignores me and opens the door to the bedroom.

We are met by a low and vicious growl.

2 CHAPTER

Fortunately, the growl is not meant for Dad or me. Kegan is trying to help Alita into bed after placing her in what sort of looks like a hospital gown from the Cowan realm. It's a loose flowing thing that ties in the back. I am going to assume Tabitha told him what to make when the time came. I doubt Kegan is thinking clearly enough at the moment to have come up with it on his own.
Unfortunately, he was so focused on getting her gown correct that Kegan wasn't paying enough attention while steering Alita to the bed. She ended up stubbing her toe on the bed frame just as we came in. Hence, the growl. She doesn't seem as angry with him as I would expect about it, though. Maybe it's because she is currently having a contraction and she is distracted from the pain in her toe by pain elsewhere.

"Let me help," Dad says, hurrying over to them. He takes Alita's other arm and helps steer her more safely toward the side of the bed. She waits until her contraction is done before climbing on. Once she is settled, Dad explains about the midwife. Kegan shoots me a worried look over my dad's shoulder.

"Don't worry, he's delivered a ton of babies," I assure the anxious dad-to-be.

Switching to doctor mode, Dad says to Alita, "I should check your progress." After the two agree, Dad does a quick exam on Alita to get an idea of where she is in terms of labor. Unfortunately, she is not very far along. "It will be hours yet," Dad informs us all.

He's right, of course. Who knew how time consuming labor and delivery could be. Not to mention boring for those of us not directly involved in the process. In the movies, women go from their water breaking to having a baby in minutes. Real life is not at all like that. And if you're not the one having painful contractions, it can be rather dull. I am not stupid enough to say that out loud, though. Good thing I've had practice keeping my mouth shut around Alita these past couple of months.

The next few hours are mostly about making the mother-to-be comfortable. Tabitha brings her a potion which takes away most of the pain of the contractions and

Alita's mood lightens considerably afterwards, much to Kegan's relief. His fear factor lowers proportionately as her pain lessens as Alita and the baby are much less likely to cause him magical harm if they are comfortable. Every once in a while, Dad checks to see how far dilated she is. The rest of the time, Kegan sits next to her on the bed doing his best to make her laugh, which is really sweet. When Alita has a contraction, he holds her hand and talks her through it. For the most part, they are both much calmer than I would have expected them to be. Kallen and I would be freaking out, I'm certain of it.

The baby, on the other hand, is not so calm and seems to be growing more agitated by the minute if the growing magic in the air is any indication. It may not be attacking its father, but it is definitely using its abilities. Tabitha suggests it is impatient to be born and is showing thus impatience with a pretty impressive magical show. Random things are floating around the room. More than once Dad needs to bat something away from his head or face as he can't use magic to dispel it. I try hard not to laugh. At least, when the small things fly at him. The bigger things I need to keep from causing him actual harm.

It becomes less funny as Alita nears delivery time. The baby is growing more and more aggressive, and I try not to see the worry lines on Tabitha's face. But, when the dresser rises a good ten inches from the floor and crashes forward, I know something is wrong. Even Dad can sense the anxiety in the magic around him. He turns to me. "Can you make me a stethoscope?"

Me? I almost squeak. Then I see a flash of pain on Alita's face and my performance anxiety disappears. A stethoscope appears in Dad's hands. He moves to the side of the bed and places the ear pieces in his ears and presses the end to Alita's stomach. He moves it around several times. Each time, his expression grows grimmer. Finally, he says to Alita and Kegan, "I don't like what I'm hearing in regards to the heartbeat. I think the cord is wrapped around the baby's neck."

Kegan turns ashen. "That is bad, right?"

Dad nods sympathetically. "Yes, that's bad. If the baby moves into the birth canal with the cord wrapped around its neck, it will strangle itself."

"Xandra, come here," Tabitha says sharply. I'm so startled by her tone that my feet start working before my mind catches up. I am already standing next to her by the time I say. "What?"

In a hushed tone, she murmurs, "The midwife would be able to ease the cord from the baby's neck with magic. I have never done it before."

I put my hands up to ward off her next words. "I've certainly never done it before. I wouldn't have the first clue what to do."

Dad has joined us. "I don't like the idea of anyone trying to do it blind. Worse comes to worst, I can do a C-section." When he gets a blank look from Tabitha, he explains, "Cut the baby out."

Tabitha waves him off. "No need to go to such extremes yet. We'll try something else first." The only problem with that is she doesn't seem to know what that something else is.

After a moment's deliberation, an idea comes to Dad. Turning to Tabitha, he asks, "Do you think you could unwind the cord if you were able to see it?" Tabitha stares at him blankly, wondering if maybe he lost his mind.

His meaning is slowly starting to sink into my brain, though. "You want me to make it possible for you to see the baby without doing a C-section." Dad nods. Great, no pressure. Turning to Tabitha, I ask, "Um, any idea how I'm supposed to do that?"

Shaking her head, Tabitha admits, "I do not have a clue." Guess there's not an existing spell for it.

Great. I glance over my shoulder to the scared couple on the bed. "Do we have time to wait for the midwife?"

Dad grimaces. "If she is delivering another baby, we have no idea how long it will take for her to arrive. It could be too late."

Alita lifts tear filled eyes to me. She and Kegan heard every word of our conversation. The room is not big enough for them not to have. "Please," she begs.

Well, there's no saying no to that plea. Squaring my shoulders, I march toward her. Hopefully by the time I get there, I'll have a clue as to what I should be doing. When I am next to the bed, I reach a hand out to lay it on Alita's stomach. Before I can touch her, Kegan grabs my wrist. "Are you certain you can do this?" There is an undercurrent to his words. A threat. If I do anything to harm his child or his wife, he will find a way to harm me.

I try really hard not to smile. I like seeing this protective side of him. It's sweet. "I will do my best," I assure him solemnly. He nods and lets go of my wrist.

I push Alita's gown aside so I can place my hand directly on the skin of her swollen belly. As soon as I touch her, the spell is there on the tip of my tongue. *"Tiny, new life faced with a hapless fate, poses the need for magic and technology to conflate. To guide a savior's hand, this precious womb must be scanned. Show us now the internal workings of nature's most wondrous blessings."*

The room was already dim. Tabitha had pulled the sheer drapes closed to keep the bright light of the sun from Alita's eyes. But now, the room grows dark as the walls around us blacken. All except one. The wall at the head of the bed begins to shine. In the light, a picture forms. It's like an old fashioned home movie playing out on the wall. And there, in the middle of the frame, is Kegan and Alita's baby inside the womb in perfect color. There also is proof that Dad is right. The umbilical cord is clearly wrapped around the baby's neck.

"That is better than an ultrasound," Dad says in wonder.

Tabitha doesn't waste any time. She bustles to the bed and lays her hands on Alita's belly, pushing mine aside in her haste. She doesn't notice and I don't mention it. I just step back and let her do her thing. The older Fairy's eyes are glued to the picture on the wall. Pulling magic, she gently sends it into the womb, guiding it toward the umbilical cord. Ever so slowly, she is able to unwind it. It feels as if it takes hours. I'm glad it doesn't because I am holding my breath the entire time and that would be bad for my necessary oxygen supply. It probably takes only a minute or so.

I would expect Kegan to be watching the wall, but his eyes are glued to Alita's. He is murmuring encouraging words and keeping her eyes focused only on him. He doesn't want her to watch in case something goes very wrong. I suspect he also knows Tabitha will be even more nervous than she already is if the parents are watching her work and gasping each time the cord moves. She already has sweat dripping down the sides of her face. I would use one of the many towels in the room to wipe it off, but I'm afraid of breaking her concentration.

There is a collective sigh of relief when Tabitha removes her hands from Alita's belly and steps back. She turns to Dad. "Check her."

Dad moves forward with the stethoscope. He repeats his process from earlier, listening to several areas. Finally, a smile breaks out on his face. "There's a strong heartbeat. The cord is clear."

"Good, because I'm pretty sure I should be pushing now," Alita declares.

Dad chuckles and checks other areas without the use of the stethoscope. "Not quite yet, but soon," he tells her and Alita grimaces. Yup, birthing babies is a long, drawn out process.

One long hour later, Dad is finally holding a very wet and slimy baby boy. "Do you want to cut the cord?" he asks Kegan as he hands the baby into the waiting arms of Tabitha who is holding a clean sheet.

Kegan blanches but replies, "Yes."

While Dad finishes up with Alita, Tabitha prepares the baby. She cleans its mouth and eyes and gets it to cry to clear its lungs. When she is finished, she hands the baby to Alita. There is not a dry eye in the room as mother gazes at baby. Kegan's especially.

"Do you have a name?" Dad asks. The pair have been amazingly tight lipped about their list of possible names.

Alita smiles. "His name is Keelan."

My brow furrows. "Is that a combination of Kegan and Kallen?"

Neither parent bothers to look up from their newborn. "Yes, that is why we chose the name," Alita says softly. "And it means warrior. He is our little warrior, just like his father and his uncle." My heart swells. Kallen is going to be so honored. No matter how much he and his cousin tease and bicker, there is a lot of love there.

Speaking of my wonderful husband, there's a light knock on the door. The crowd that has been waiting in the hall must have heard the baby crying. Smiling, I ask the proud parents, "Are you ready to show off baby Keelan?"

Kegan nods. "Let them in."

I open the door and several people practically fall through it since they were all crowded against the wood. Isla is the first to enter, followed by Kallen, Mom, Adriel, Raziel, Dagda, Tana, Garren and Alita's parents. They circle the bed, waiting to be invited closer. Reluctantly, Alita relinquishes her new son to Kegan's hands. He stands and hands him to his grandmother first.

Isla beams at her great-grandson. She leans down and kisses his smooth brow. "You are the handsomest baby I have ever seen."

"I will not take that personally," a voice drawls from the doorway. We all turn toward him. Kegan's father is standing there, not quite sure if he is welcome to cross the threshold. He and Kegan have not really spoken since the older Fairy demanded Kegan and Alita come live with him when he found out his grandchild would be strong magically. The new parents chose to stay with us, instead. I wonder who sent him a message about the birth. I suspect Isla. I know Kallen wouldn't have done it. Not without asking Kegan first. My eyes fly to the new father for a sign that I should send his father packing. I get a slight shake of the head from Kegan. He can stay.

Part of me is disappointed since he generally causes nothing but grief for the couple. I guess they are too happy at the moment to care about any of that. Who knows, maybe they can move past it all someday soon.

Kegan retrieves his son from Isla and nods to his father who takes several tentative steps closer. He is not quite ready to hold his grandson, though. "I might drop him," he insists when Kegan attempts to hand his son to him. I narrow my eyes and study him, trying to determine if he is serious or not. I believe he is genuinely afraid he will drop the tiny Fairy.

Dad, still in doctor mode, announces to the room in general, "Alita needs her rest. Perhaps a few minutes with the grandparents, but the rest of us should give them some privacy."

I am about to suggest that I stay behind and help clean up when Tabitha performs an amazing act of magic. The sheets on the bed are suddenly clean and dry. All the soiled linens have been collected in a laundry bag, including the ones used to keep the mattress from getting wet and gross during the birth. Alita is dressed in a fresh gown and her hair and skin have been magically cleansed. She is ready for a peaceful night with her new child. The room next door was converted to a nursery long ago with an adjoining door in the parents' room and it is ready for its tiny new occupant. There is nothing left to do at the moment. So, all of us not in the grandparent category reluctantly shuffle out of the room, everyone trying to get one last peek at Keelan before we go.

In the hall, Kallen wraps an arm around my waist and pulls me close. "How was it?"

"We are never having children," I inform him emphatically.

3 CHAPTER

Hunger drives us all downstairs. It is well past dinnertime. In the kitchen, Mom and Dad begin pulling items out for sandwiches. Kallen and I gather plates and knives. Raziel and Dagda pull items from the pantry to go with the sandwiches. Everything is stacked in the middle of the island counter buffet style. "Dig in," Mom announces when everything is set.

When our plates are piled high, all conversation turns toward the new baby. Details of the birth are requested. I oblige but leave out the gorier parts that would make some in the room not want to finish their sandwiches. Including me if I think too hard about them. Dad tells of the makeshift ultrasound I created, and Dagda is fascinated by the idea. They spend several minutes discussing the usefulness of the magic with Dagda trying to figure out if the magic was too complex for the average

Fairy midwife to perform. I personally don't have a clue but offer to try to teach them the spell.

"Was it really that bad?" Kallen finally asks when he can get my undivided attention. "Do you really not want to experience it for yourself?" There is disappointment lurking in his eyes, but also resolve. If I say I don't want children, he will accept that.

I smile and touch his cheek. "I want children someday. But, I don't think any woman ever watches the birth of a child and says, 'wow, I want to do that right now!'"

Kallen chuckles. "As I have never witnessed a birth, I must take your word for it." He pulls me into a hug. "We will not even discuss having a child of our own until the trauma of your experience leaves your mind."

"And then we'll add a few years to that," I inform him, not wanting him to get any ideas of starting a family in the near future. "We have a lot to accomplish before we can even think about having kids. Life is too dangerous around me still."

The kitchen door bursts open. "Is the baby here?" Zac demands, sliding to a halt on the kitchen tile. He is just returning from the palace and training.

Dad ruffles his sandy brown hair. "He sure is. Alita is resting right now, but maybe I can take you up later when I check on her."

"How were your lessons today?" Mom asks.

Zac makes a face. "I never get to do any good magic in my lessons."

Dagda cocks a brow, slightly offended since he is the one who devises the lesson plans for the tutors to follow. "What would be considered 'good magic?'"

Shrugging as he grabs for a piece of turkey, Zac replies, "I want to learn to do the things Xandra can do, like toss people across the room."

My biological father gives me an annoyed glance before turning back to Zac. "Though that is a useful skill in battle, there is not a lot of practical use for it on a day to day basis." He shoots me another annoyed look. Geez. Send a few people through walls and suddenly you're a bad influence. "You also must learn the basics before you can train as a warrior."

With a long-suffering sigh, Zac pouts, "I guess." He pops the turkey into his mouth.

"How about if I make you a sandwich?" Mom says before he can grab another piece of meat. "And you can wash your hands before eating it." Her tone is firm but her eyes are twinkling. She loves being able to do things for him again. Even something as simple as making him a sandwich for dinner even though I suspect my younger brother already had dinner at the palace.

Isla and Garren enter the room, both grinning like proud new great-grandparents. "Why don't we have a bonfire on the beach to celebrate," Garren suggests as he begins making sandwiches for himself and Isla. The latter pours them both a cup of coffee.

"Excellent suggestion," someone responds and several others agree. It's decided.

Kallen and I head out to the beach to get things going while the others stay behind to clean up the kitchen. Kallen creates a small fire pit in the sand and I gather wood from the bin near the house. There are several fireplaces in the mansion so we always have a supply of firewood on hand. Kallen uses the wood I bring him to make a decent size fire.

We are soon joined by the others who are bearing various beverages. There's wine, coffee and lemonade available, as well as a few treats Tabitha made earlier in the day before Alita went into labor. Beach chairs are created and we settle in to watch the fire and listen to stories.

Dagda tells tales of battles won by the Fairies over the years. Isla's stories focus around family history. Tabitha's stories are about helping to raise the King and Kallen and Kegan. Hers are the funniest. Tana tells stories of her life before becoming Queen, and about what it's like to be married to the King which can, on occasion, be quite trying apparently. There is humor and love in her stories, though. None of them include the dark past they share, thank goodness. Mom and Dad tell stories of life in the Cowan realm. Mom talks about growing up as a Witch, and Dad tells stories of his exploits in college. Even Adriel gets involved, telling us some of the more interesting beings she has encountered as an Angel of Death. She is careful not to give away any Angel secrets out of fear for her wings. All in all, it is a great night.

Our little party finally breaks up when Kegan signals us from the doorway of the terrace. He has brought Keelan down to say good night to everyone, but he doesn't want to bring him out into the night air. So, the fire is extinguished and we all spend several minutes in the large living room gushing over the beautiful baby in his arms. Tana and Mom are both eager to hold him so the rest of us hang back and give them space. Dagda takes his turn and I smile at the sight. It makes me wish he and Tana had been able to have children together. Being who he is now, not the angry King who was bitter over a stupid feud with a Witch when I was conceived, I suspect he could be a great father to a young child. He does an excellent job with Zac.

Pulling me aside, Kallen wraps his arms around me and kisses me. "Ready for bed?"

I nod and yawn at the same time. "Definitely."

"Let's sneak away then."

I briefly consider how rude it is not to say good night to everyone, but decide I am too tired to care. Besides, they are too enthralled by the baby to even notice we are gone. "Let's go." Holding tight to my gorgeous husband, I teleport us to our bedroom. Once there, I make sure the door is closed before teleporting us directly to the bed. Kallen chuckles as we topple on top of it. "That eager for sleep?" he asks, pulling me closer.

"That eager for you," I purr, kissing him deeply. I may not want to get pregnant yet, but I am certainly up for the practice.

Rolling us onto our sides, Kallen pulls back slightly and tucks a strand of dark hair behind my ear. "I am immensely happy. I would not change a thing about our life together."

I smile. "Me, either. I was so lonely growing up, and now we have this huge family who love us and we love them. I couldn't be happier. Even if all of us living together in the same house does drive me crazy from time to time," I add with a laugh.

Kissing me softly, Kallen says, "Yes, the interruptions on our privacy have tried my nerves from time to time." He pulls me close again, making our clothes disappear in the process.

I roll him over onto his back, my hands roving over his taut muscles and bare skin. "I don't think anyone is going to interrupt us tonight." I cover his body with mine, reveling in the skin to skin contact.

The time for words has passed. I kiss his lips passionately before letting my mouth and hands wander over the rest of his incredible body. I savor every touch and every sensation, longing for this night to last forever. My desire for him is eternal, just as his is for me. Never will we know anything different.

And doesn't that just make the universe perfect.

4 CHAPTER

Why can't mornings come later? Or weekly. Mornings should come weekly. That way, I could spend days making love to my husband, and then get more than an hour or two of sleep before mornings come along and ruin everything. Then again, is it really morning's fault that I have a Tasmanian devil sitting on my chest breathing bacon fumes into my nostrils? Not really.

Shoving at the fat little beast, I mumble, "Get off me." Since I am only able to push him partially off, I decide he is going on a strict, no more than five pieces of bacon a day, diet.

"Something is wrong."

I scowl at Taz. "What do you mean, something is wrong?"

"The brat is gone."

It takes a moment for the words to sink into my sleep addled brain. When they do, I sit up so fast, Taz goes tumbling off the side of the bed. "Keelan?"

Righting himself, Taz snarls up at me from the floor, "Do you know of any other brats in the house?"

I consider telling him that I am looking at one, but I need to find out more about what is going on with Keelan. "How do you know he's gone?" I ask. I glance over my shoulder at Kallen who is beginning to stir. I don't want to wake him until I know more. No sense in both of us panicking yet.

"Because Alita's gone, too."

"What?!"

My shriek is so loud, Kallen is sitting up now. So much for not waking him yet. "What's wrong?" he demands, sleep erased from his face in a flash.

I turn to him. "Taz says Alita and Keelan are gone!"

Confusion washes over my husband's features. "Who is Keelan?" he asks.

Did he already forget the baby's name? "Keelan, Alita and Kegan's new baby," I remind him, trying to be patient. He did just wake up. But really, how could he forget the baby's name? Keelan was partially named after him.

Kallen's confusion deepens a moment before slowly converting to humor. "You had me going for a minute." He stretches and yawns. "It is not like you to wake me up so abruptly to tease me, though. I believe I will need to get revenge." He reaches out and wraps his arms around me, pulling me back to the bed. "Later. For now, how about if we begin the morning again." He moves to kiss me but I am too shocked to let him.

I struggle out of his arms and sit back up. My own confusion doesn't morph into amusement; it goes straight to anger. "That's all you have to say about Alita and Keelan being gone?"

Propping himself on his elbows, Kallen studies me for a minute. It finally dawns on him how angry I am. His words are slow and careful when he speaks, trying hard not to piss me off even more. "I assume that Alita is home with her parents where she is every night. And if she and my cousin had a child together, Grandmother certainly would have insisted upon a hand-fasting quite some time ago."

My mouth falls open. I cannot make words. My vocal cords are in shock. Kallen reaches a hand up to feel my forehead to see if I'm feverish and I slap his hand away. I still can't speak, though.

"Xandra? Are you okay?"

Finally, my will to speak dominates the shock affecting my body. "They *are* hand-fasted," I growl.

"I can't believe the wanker thinks this is a good time to try to grow a sense of humor," Taz grumbles. He has rejoined us on the bed. "Even I know when to stop trying to piss you off."

Taz is right. This isn't like Kallen, who now seems to be in his own shocked stupor. I stare more closely at my husband and I get an epiphany. I'm not feeling any tingling sensation on my skin which would indicate he's not being one hundred percent honest. "He isn't joking. He really doesn't know they're hand-fasted," I whisper to Taz.

"Did you push him out of bed and he hit his head?" Taz asks. "I wouldn't blame you if you did, he is a wanker, after all."

I scowl at my Familiar. "No, I did not push him out of bed."

"Me or the beast?" Kallen asks suspiciously.

"Never mind." I reach out a hand to touch *his* forehead to see if he's warm. "Are you feeling okay?"

It's Kallen's turn to scowl and he pushes my hand away. More gently than I did his. "I feel fine. I am not the one who has my cousin and Alita married off and reproducing."

That's it, something is definitely wrong. Maybe Isla or Tabitha can shed some light on what's going on with him. I don't sense any magic that could be affecting him, so maybe Taz is right. Maybe during the night Kallen hit his head and suddenly has selective amnesia or something. I better get Dad involved, too, just in case this is a medical, not magical, thing. Throwing back the covers, I get out of bed. "Come on."

Kallen lays back and stretches languorously, not in the same hurry I am to get this resolved. "My love, you probably had a dream that has stuck with you. The certainty of it will pass soon. More sleep will help. Come back to bed."

I gape at him. "A dream? You think I dreamed Alita and Kegan getting married, her pregnancy and the birth of their child yesterday?"

His response is immediate. "Yes."

"Get out of bed," I growl. We are going to settle this once and for all.

Reluctantly, Kallen rises. "Not the way I intended to start the morning," he grumbles as he dresses himself. I am so annoyed, I barely notice his hard, muscled body before he covers it with clothes. Barely. Okay, I'm not dead and he's gorgeous. Of course I ogle him. He catches me and a smug grin covers his face. I glower at him which only makes him chuckle.

I throw on a pair of jeans and a t-shirt from my drawers. I don't want Kallen to dress me in case there is something wrong with him which could also affect his magic. I would rather not end up naked in the middle of the kitchen if his magic goes awry. When we are both dressed, I grab his hand and pull him from the room and down the stairs. He comes willingly, but his concern over my mental health seems to be growing considering the odd looks he's throwing my way. Well, the feeling is mutual for once.

In the kitchen, we find Isla and Tabitha enjoying a cup of coffee. It isn't a work day, so Isla is not getting ready to rush off to the palace. I will have her undivided attention. She looks up when we enter the room. "Good morning. You two have risen early."

I don't bother with niceties. "Will you please inform your grandson that Kegan and Alita are indeed married and just had a child named Keelan yesterday?"

I have never seen Tabitha spew coffee from her nose before. It's rather disgusting. And painful from the looks of it. I bet it was hot coffee. That cannot be good for the mucus membranes. "What?!" she sputters.

Isla is calmer about it. "Xandra, dear, whatever are you talking about?" Calmer, not saner apparently.

What is wrong with everyone? Maybe if I say it slower. This time, I enunciate each word carefully. "I am talking about Keelan. Your great-grandson. Born yesterday."

Isla looks past me to Kallen. "How long has she been having this delusion?"

"Delusion??" If I was drinking coffee, it would be spewing through my nose at the moment. Maybe even my eyeballs. "I am not delusional!"

Pursing her lips, Isla studies me for a moment before turning to Tabitha. "Does she seem unwell to you?"

Tabitha's voice comes out nasally after searing her mucus membranes with hot coffee. "She is spouting nonsense and growing more agitated by the second. I would not call that well."

"What is wrong with everyone?" Taz asks from near my ankle echoing my thoughts from a moment ago. He's too upset to even make a snarky comment. Things are bad indeed if that has happened.

"I don't know," I whisper, growing more worried by the second.

My other Familiar comes strolling into the room. "Ah, you are awake. Has my insane friend here told you what he believes has occurred between Kallen's cousin and the young Fairy from down the beach?"

My eyes shoot from Taz to Felix and then back to Taz. "He doesn't believe it either?" Then another thought hits me and I narrow my eyes. "And you didn't tell me he didn't believe it before I came down here? You could have given me a heads up that whatever this is has affected the whole house, not just Kallen."

"I did not know it affected the entire house," Taz denies, but the creepy-crawlies on my skin make it very clear he is lying.

Placing a protective arm around my waist, Kallen pulls my attention from Taz and says gently, "Perhaps I should invite my cousin over so he can confirm that he is not hand-fasted."

This is getting weirder by the second. "Invite him over? He's upstairs in his room, isn't he?"

"Kegan did not stay here last night," Isla says, concern radiating from her. Turning to Kallen, she orders, "Send him a message and insist he come right over."

The kitchen door opens and Garren comes in with Dad. They have been fishing, obviously, as the latter is carrying a string of fish native to the area. "Dad!" I am so happy to see him, I rush over and give him a hug.

"Good morning," he chuckles after the initial surprise of me hugging him fish and all wears off. "You are certainly exuberant this morning."

Stepping back, I jump right in. "Dad, tell them you helped deliver Alita's baby yesterday."

Dad's eyes grow round and he glances over my head to Kallen. I turn just in time to see my husband shrug helplessly. Dad brings his attention back to me. "Xandra, are you feeling alright?"

I'm getting tired of that question. Instead of responding, I turn to my husband with my hands firmly planted on my hips. "Did you send Kegan a message yet?"

Eying me warily, Kallen nods. "I did."

"Fine. I'll be outside until he gets here. Come on, Taz."

"But, Mama Bacon is getting ready to cook," my Familiar whines.

"Taz!" Maybe because I sound like I'm holding onto the last frayed strings of my sanity, or maybe because I've accidently pulled enough magic to pluck each one of his hairs out individually and painfully, whichever it is, my Familiar trots after me. Grumbling and irritated though he is.

I leave the house through the terrace doors and stomp down the steps to the beach. "Is this a joke? Are they playing some elaborate prank? If so, I don't think it's very funny."

"Felix is not much for jokes. Believe me, I've tried," Taz grouses.

I stop and look down at him. "It is weird that Felix is involved." I could see him being talked into remaining quiet about a prank if he thought it was harmless. But, actively participating? Especially in one that is so obviously driving me insane? It doesn't add up.

"There must be some kind of spell," Taz offers.

I shake my head. "I don't sense any magic, do you?"

"Maybe the Angels are up to something?"

With a sigh, I start walking again. "Could be. But to what end? Why would the Angels care if Kegan and Alita are hand-fasted or not?" My heart clenches and I stop walking. Wide eyed with fear, I ask, "Do you think Keelan is okay?"

Taz sits on his haunches. "I've been thinking about that."

"You have?" I ask dubiously. He rarely thinks about anything other than his stomach. He is behaving strangely and it's freaking me out. I can't help but ask, "Why aren't you being all snarky with me this morning?" Then it hits me. "You're scared."

Taz shoots to his feet, his little tail high in the air. "Scared you're keeping me from my morning bacon," he sniffs, obviously offended by my declaration.

I wave off his defensiveness and get back to what's more important at the moment. "You said you've been thinking about what happened to Keelan. What conclusion did you come to?"

My charming Familiar turns his butt toward me and starts walking back to the house. "I don't care to share my ideas with you."

I roll my eyes at his poutiness. "Taz, knock it off. We need to figure this out. Tell me what you've been thinking. Please."

After a second, he stops waddling forward. Turning, his beady black eyes meet my green ones. "What if we've been having a shared vision of the future?"

Well, that wasn't what I expected him to say. "You think the past year or two has all been an elaborate vision of the future?"

He cocks his little head to the side. "Obviously my vision of your stupidity was accurate." There's the Taz I know and often despise. Before I can tell him this, he continues. "Last night. I believe we had the vision about Kegan and Alita last night. And it was so detailed, we feel like it already happened."

"Do you really believe that?" I scoff. I know I don't.

Up ahead on the terrace, Kallen is waving to us. "Wanker alert," Taz mutters under his breath.

With a sigh, I step forward. "Let's go. Kegan must be here." That was fast. Kallen's message must have indicated an emergency.

"Woo hoo, two wankers for the price of one."

I'd be annoyed with my Familiar, but I'm not feeling too friendly about anyone in the house at the moment. I'm going to let the wanker statement stand. Only in my mind, of course, and I'm increasing it to include everyone currently in the house. Not very charitable of me, but I don't really care at the moment.

5 CHAPTER

"Hand-fasted?" Kegan gulps. "Me?"

If he didn't look so utterly terrified at the thought, I would think he was in on the prank. But, he's not that good of an actor. I don't even need my supernatural lie detecting skill. If this was a joke, he'd be having trouble hiding a grin. His eyes wouldn't be darting toward the door ready to make his escape so this difficult and embarrassing, for both him and me now, conversation will come to an abrupt end.

I can't let it drop, though. "Have you asked Alita to marry you?" I push. Maybe Taz is right. Maybe he and I had a joint vision of the future. I don't really believe that, but what else could it be?

Kegan's skin is a deep shade of rust at the moment. "Alita and I are not that close."

I mentally wire my jaw closed so I don't say anything else which is going to make everyone think I'm crazier than they already believe. I imagine the metal lacing into the bones and between my teeth, and then the sharp tug that binds everything together tightly. For good measure, I imagine my lips being sewn together. I imagine it so well they actually sting a bit. Oh, that's because I'm biting them. I relax my teeth slightly before I draw blood. I have so many questions I want, and need, to ask. I do not want, or need, everyone in the room who is staring at me like I'm crazy to haul me off to a padded room, though. What I need to do is step back and assess the situation. Figure out what is really happening before I convince everyone that I truly am insane. Whatever is going on, it is clear that Taz and I have a completely different idea of reality than everyone else.

The kitchen door opens and my biological father strolls in. He has obviously been informed of what is going on because he heads straight for me. Placing his hands on my cheeks, he moves my head from side to side, assessing me for magic and whatnot. Over my head, he asks Kallen, "How is she?"

"She is fine," I grumble, pulling my face from his hands.

Ignoring me, Dagda turns his attention to Tabitha. "Can anything be done for her?"

"Um, I'm not dying," I inform him. He completely ignores me again.

A general discussion begins in the room regarding my physical and psychological health. None of it is directed toward me. I am about to comment on that when there is a sharp pain at my ankle. I glare down at my Familiar who just bit me. "What was that for?"

"Just making sure you are still here. No one else seems to be able to see you. Wanted to make sure I'm not as crazy as they think you are." My response is to kick out at him, but despite his extra body fat, Taz is pretty spry when he wants to be. He easily avoids my foot.

Honestly, though, I shouldn't be too mean to him. After all, he is the only one who believes me. "I'm leaving," I tell Taz. "No one will even notice."

"I will notice," a deep voice behind me says. Kallen slips his hands around my waist and leans his chin on my head.

My first instinct is to cuddle into him, pull his arms tighter around me and try to forget what is going on. Then I remember that he doesn't believe me, either. So instead, I step forward out of his embrace. "I'm going back outside. I need some fresh air."

"I will come with you," Kallen insists. Out of a strong desire for my company, or to keep me from harming myself and others? I'm not sure which.

Either way, I don't want him to come along. "No, you stay here and try to figure out what's wrong with me." I know I sound whiny and miserable, but I just can't help it. I am miserable. I feel like I'm six and being told that Santa Claus doesn't really exist. Not an analogy I am going to share with the crowd in the kitchen, though. Bringing up a mythical creature whom I thought was real for a number of years past the age of six would probably not go a long way in regards to proving my state of mental fitness. Maybe I am crazy. Because I am positive a baby I helped in a small way to bring into this world strong and healthy is suddenly gone. A baby all of us have been eagerly anticipating for months. And I am the only one feeling its loss. Well, Taz is feeling the loss, but I'm not sure how deeply. A couple of strips of bacon and I'm sure Keelan will be completely pushed from his mind.

I am so frustrated I am having trouble controlling my magic. I need to get out of here. Turning, I slip out of the kitchen unnoticed by the others. I appreciate that Kallen doesn't come after me. I need time alone to try to wrap my mind around what is going on and to come up with possible explanations. I briefly toss around the idea of going to Angel time to seek answers, but I know I won't get any. No use in frustrating myself even further.

I wander along the beach for over an hour. I have no particular destination in mind. I was tempted to go to the beach home of Alita's parents, but decided against it. If Kegan doesn't know they're hand-fasted, I hold out no hope that Alita does. Not to mention, it seems cruel to tell her she had a baby yesterday but I have no idea what happened to it. No, it's best to avoid her for the time being.

After another hour, hunger starts to gnaw at my gut. I'm not ready to go back yet, though, so I ignore it. Glancing around, I realize I'm quite far from the house and may actually be lost. Considering the fact that I can teleport, I don't fret much about it. I do plop down in the sand to rest my feet. Pulling my knees up, I wrap my arms around my legs and stare out over the ocean, hoping to find some peace.

"A soul so lost I've never before found, the oppressive weight of her melancholy astounds. What blow could be dealt so cruelly, to devastate this one so truly? For certainly this one could not be hell bound."

My head is whipping back and forth as I search for the speaker of the terrible rhyme. A deep growl to my left lowers my eyes from the tree line to the sand. Taz, who has been unnaturally silent during our walk, probably because he is too weak from not having eaten in two hours to speak, is snarling at something. Peering around him, I half expect to find a Pixie. What else is small enough to be blocked by Taz's body but still able to speak?

Well, it seems the need for concern over my state of mental wellbeing may not be as exaggerated as I thought. Because it is not a Pixie in the sand. It is a crab. A bright red, huge clawed crab. And I am one hundred percent convinced it spoke the rhyme.

I shake my head and laugh. Am I seriously considering the idea that a crab just spoke to me? Well, not to me, really. More about me. In rhyme. Yup, I'm insane. I nudge Taz with my foot. "Leave the crab alone."

"The little twit wad can speak," Taz growls.

Oh, he heard it, too? With a long suffering sigh, I say to my Familiar. "I think there's something wrong with us, Taz. It's not them, it's us. We're the ones with the problem."

"The girl speaks in riddles not meant to confuse. Yet this poor crab knows not what to muse. Tis it kismet or fate on this strange date that has brought me so far beyond my ability to purview?"

Taz cranes his neck so he can stare up at me. "You heard that, right?"

I nod slowly. "The terrible use of purview as a rhyme with muse, yes, I heard it."

Taz plops down on his haunches, the crab completely forgotten for the moment. "You are taking this rather calmly. Has all the stuffing been removed from your brain and replaced with straw as I've long suspected?"

"I'm hearing a crab speak in terrible rhymes and you think I'm going to be bothered by your insults? Besides, you hear him, too, and you're not exactly freaking out about it."

Taz looks from me, to the crab, to the tree line behind us. "We could drag a bit of wood over here for a fire and have crab legs for breakfast. That would solve our immediate problem."

I purse my lips and shake my head. "I've never really liked crab."

"He's small. I didn't really want to share anyway." Taz starts walking toward the trees. "I'll be right back." I assume he is going for firewood.

"I won't really let him eat you," I assure the crab. Great, now I'm speaking to him. Her? I open my mouth to ask which gender it is, but snap it closed again. Does it make me crazier asking the talking crab whether it is male or female? In the big picture, does it really matter?

"Tis good to know fairest of the Fae, that my life knows no danger today. In case your pet does not know this yet, I shall now disappear into the ocean's spray." The crab scurries across the sand and disappears into the water as promised.

I glance back over my shoulder to see Taz dragging a rather large stick my way. "We are not having crab legs for lunch," I inform him. "He left."

Disgusted, he drops the stick to the ground. "One little crab. You couldn't manage to snare one little crab? You do know you have magic, right? It can be used for such things."

I tilt my head and ask, "Would you really eat a talking crab?"

"Yes." I believe him. "Or we could have at least brought it back with us."

"I considered that, but everyone already thinks I'm crazy. Insisting I caught a talking crab doesn't seem like the best way to prove that I'm not."

"But it actually spoke," Taz points out in slow, measured words as if I'm an imbecile.

"Did it?" I counter. "Did it really?" It could just be another joint delusion. Since he doesn't seem to know how to respond, I change the subject. "I think we need a new approach. Obviously, there is something going on and we're not going to figure it out on the beach far away from everyone. We need to go home."

"Where they want to put you in a straitjacket and force feed you Jell-O? Good plan." Because Taz is a part of me, created from my psyche, he understands references to things from my old world even though he never lived there.

"Yeah, we need to convince them not to do that."

"Wow, you really are a brainiac."

Ignoring his snide comment, I continue. "We need to convince them that we don't actually believe that Kegan and Alita are married."

"We? They have no idea what I believe since the only one who can understand me is you. You'll be locked in the crazy room all by yourself."

"Felix knows," I point out. Taz's little shoulders slump in defeat and he doesn't interrupt again. "We'll tell them what you suggested earlier. That I've developed a new power. The ability to see the future."

"And your first vision was so powerful that you couldn't discern it from reality," Taz nods, growing to like the idea. "They are big enough morons to actually believe it."

"Watch it." My family may think I'm crazy at the moment, but they are still my family and I'm feeling guilty about calling them wankers earlier. Even if it was just in my head. Standing up, I glance at the water trying to catch a glimpse of red. No such luck. The crab is gone. "Come on, let's go home."

"Alright, but there had better be some bacon left over from breakfast," Taz grumbles. "I'm not starving myself over this insanity."

6 Chapter

I teleport us to the beach in front of the terrace. I am not surprised to find Kallen there pacing. He turns worried eyes to me as soon as he senses my presence. In a wary voice, he asks, "How are you?"

I paste a bright smile to my face. "Not crazy, how are you?"

"I never thought you were crazy," he assures me. Surprisingly, he means it. I don't feel a trace of a lie in his words. "I am simply worried there is something going on which we have not figured out yet."

I nod in agreement. "There is." I brace myself to tell an out and out lie to my husband. Good thing he's not a walking lie detector. "I believe I have a new power." I feel dirty and deceitful lying to him. I am seriously going to have to find a way to make this up to him after I figure out what the hell is going on.

I am not the most convincing liar, so it is not surprising when my husband stares at me doubtfully. "A new power?"

"What might this new power be?" Dagda asks from the doorway. How does he always manage to make dramatic entrances? Must be his special Fairy talent. His annoying special Fairy talent.

Squaring my shoulders, I bolster my courage to tell lie number two. "I believe I can see the future."

Dagda is as dubious as Kallen was. "You are a seer now?"

I nod and attempt to explain what I suspect is going to be a complicated lie to maintain. "I believe I saw a possible future for Kegan and Alita. Since it was my first vision and a powerful one, I confused it with reality. How was I to know I suddenly gained a new talent?"

Neither of them are willing to believe me yet. I glance down at Taz and find him inching away from me. That certainly doesn't help my case. I catch his eye and glower at him, and he reluctantly moves closer to me once more. We are in this together whether he likes it or not.

"What is this of a new talent?" Isla asks from behind Dagda. She must have heard our voices.

"Xandra claims she can see the future," Dagda explains, his eyes never leaving mine as his gaze bores into me. What, does he think if he drills deep enough with his eyes he'll peel back my soul like a banana and find the truth in the center? Could happen, I suppose. That's kind of what Tabitha does with her ability to see into souls.

To my great surprise, Isla isn't immediately disbelieving of the idea. Instead, she comes out onto the terrace and points to one of the chairs at the table. "Sit," she orders. "Explain."

With dread giving me feet that feel like coconuts, round, heavy and sloshy all at the same time, which makes walking much more difficult, I slowly make my way up the terrace steps to the indicated chair. I sit. I explain. I explain in great detail the courtship and eventual hand-fasting of Kegan and Alita that I saw in my 'vision'. I explain the pregnancy and the magic the baby wields. I explain the birth and the magic I used to essentially create an ultrasound. They wanted details, I give them details. More than they ever imagined possible, I assume. When I am done, a thick silence has descended over the terrace. Since I have been speaking for the last half an hour, I wait for someone else to cut through it.

Isla is first. "That is quite a lot of detail."

I nod. "Which is why I thought it was real."

She's doing the peel your soul like a banana thing with her eyes now like Dagda did earlier. I pretend not to notice. Finally, Isla says, "My visions are also quite detailed. When I first began having them, it was difficult sometimes to determine if they were memories or visions. I often did not know if they had already occurred or were simply possibilities. Of course," she adds, "I was six at the time."

I cock my head and quirk a brow. "Was there an insult in there somewhere?"

A slight smile touches her lips. "If so, it was unintentional."

"Sure it was," Taz snickers and I nudge him with my foot. Hard. He grumbles awful words in my direction and escapes into the house in search of food.

"At any age, I am certain it would be disconcerting," Isla continues, her expression thoughtful.

"You truly believe she now has the sight as you do?" Dagda asks her. Doubt is still lingering in his eyes like a dog unwilling to give up its favorite bone.

Rising from the chair she took across from me, Isla replies, "We shall see." With that cryptic remark, she heads back into the house.

Kallen reaches over and takes my hand. "I am sorry I was not more sympathetic this morning. It must have been frightening believing the world had changed so much in a day."

Yes, it certainly was. And it hasn't stopped yet. I refrain from making this comment aloud, though. After all, I have deceit to keep up. "I'll get used to it," I assure him with a forced smile. Actually, I have no intention of getting used to it. I intend to figure out what is going on and put things back to normal. I have simply bought myself some time and freedom to do the necessary investigating. It is a shame that investigating is not really a talent of mine. Kallen is better at it, I think ruefully. He won't be much help this time, though.

A wicked grin spreads across Kallen's face. "Come on out, cousin. No need to hide anymore. Xandra will not have you married off to anyone in the next hour or so."

Kegan comes through the terrace door muttering something I am glad I can't quite understand. He stops his muttering when Dagda cocks a brow in his direction. I think in his annoyance with Kallen he forgot the King was there. "I was not hiding," he says in a louder voice.

Kallen snorts. "No, merely daydreaming about how you wish it was all true." I try to hide a smirk. He probably was. Wait, it is all true. Of course Kegan wants it, and why would I mock him for it? I want it all to happen again, too.

"Hand-fasted and a father? At my age? Ridiculous," Kegan scoffs. "Why would I shackle myself like that when I am so young? I am not an idiot." He gives Kallen a pointed look.

"Hey!" I exclaim. It was not just Kallen he insulted there.

Realizing this, color rushes to Kegan's face. "Sorry," he mutters.

With a chuckle, Dagda rises. "I will leave you to sort this out on your own." Before he disappears into the house, he adds over his shoulder, "If you have more visions, I want to hear about them immediately." Of course he does.

"Sure," I reply half-heartedly. There will be no more visions, as I am not truly psychic, so it's kind of hard to get excited about it.

Frowning, Dagda stresses, "I mean it."

"Uh huh." Realizing he isn't going to get a better response, Dagda leaves the terrace. The dog with the doubt bone is still in his eyes and my tepid response isn't helping. Too bad. All I needed to do was buy time. I am not going to build this farce up any more than I need to.

Kegan plops down in a chair and stretches his legs out. "You do not seem very excited about having the sight."

I shrug. "Seems like a bother more than anything."

It begins with a deep rumbling. My chair begins to shake as does the table in front of me. The terrace itself trembles. I turn worried eyes to Kallen who is already out of his seat and staring out over the ocean. I jump to my feet next to him. "What's happening?"

"I am not certain," he claims, but I am unconvinced. He has an idea of what is going on.

"What do you think is happening?" I press.

His eyes dart to me and then back to the sea. "I do not want to alarm you without due cause."

I'm getting more frustrated by the second as the terrace continues to sway beneath our feet. The whole structure is getting stress cracks from the motion. The house behind us is moaning as it too begins to sway. "I'm already alarmed."

Muttering a foul curse under his breath which takes me a second to realize is not intended for me, Kallen pulls magic. A lot of magic. My eyes follow his and I understand. Several foul curses leave my own mouth as I pull my magic. A lot of it.

I feel the terrace fill up behind us. More importantly, I feel their magic. I hear Mom's frantic words to Dad, "Take Zac and run!" I don't turn around to see if he does as he's told. I think he will. He knows Mom needs to stay and throw her magic in with ours now that she can. It is more important for him to make sure Zac is safe than stay here with us.

"Can we stop it?" I ask Kallen.

"We will certainly try."

"Alita," Kegan says softly, the pain in his voice piercing my heart. Her parents' cottage on the shore will likely not survive this. I reach a hand out to comfort him but he is already gone, tearing down the beach in that direction. I don't try to stop him. There isn't time.

Geology was never my best subject, but even I now understand what the rumbling and shaking is all about. Somewhere, deep under the ocean, a volcano has likely erupted. "Join hands!" I call to the others. "We need to link our magic if we have any hope of stopping this!"

They do as I demand. Kallen's hand is firmly grasping my right one and Isla has taken hold of the left. The others line up, clasping each other tightly, joining us as a single unit to fight Mother Nature. Out of all the foes I've come across, I'll admit it. She is the most frightening.

The tsunami is easily a thousand feet tall and stretches as far as the eye can see in either direction. It doesn't take a genius to determine the amount of destruction it will cause. The village will be leveled. Fairies will die. The powerful may be able to save themselves and hopefully some of those around them, but many, many Fairies will die. I can't let that happen.

Tightening my hold on the hands in mine, I focus on the wave. It would be impossible to build a wall of magic tall enough and wide enough to block it. When it comes to pitting magic against natural disasters, natural disasters generally win. The only thing I can think to do is diffuse it as much as possible. I rack my brain, trying to come up with a spell.

When it comes to me, I shout it toward the water ready to devour us. *"Land and sea ready to converge, innocent lives taken when submerged. Mother Nature's rage come to life, lashing out causing peril and strife. Let our magic temper this water storm, let the particles of sand rise uniform. Stand together against nature's beast. A solid structure from west to east. Create a barrier much too difficult to mount, reduce this destructive wave to a gentle fount."*

Even before the last word of the spell has left my tongue, the sand particles are stacking themselves one upon another. Binding themselves, fusing as one. Within seconds, they have piled themselves into a massive wall which stretches as far to the left and right as the eye can see. It's going to work. It's going to stop the tsunami. Or, at least, slow it done.

Only…it doesn't.

7 CHAPTER

The last thing I remember is the water crashing through the flimsy wall of sand. What was I thinking? How could a skinny wall of sand keep millions of tons of water at bay? I don't know if it was really that much, but does it matter? It was a lot of water. And it all came down upon us. My last thought as my body was crushed beneath the water was that I at least I got to die holding onto Kallen. That's when I lost consciousness.

Now, my eyes pop open and I sit upright. "The tsunami!" I shout, ready to defend myself against mother nature again.

The sun is so bright, it takes a moment for my eyes to adjust. I expect to find myself on the beach, or amidst a pile of rubble that used to be the mansion. But, no. I'm in bed. My and Kallen's bed. Our room is still intact and the sun is streaming through the windows. Did the spell work after all?

Rubbing sleep from his eyes, Kallen rolls over. "The tsunami? What strange dream were you having?" he yawns.

Dream? My head twists back and forth searching for signs of wreckage. I did not dream the tsunami. I know I didn't. Just like I didn't dream Kegan and Alita being hand-fasted. Wait. Maybe it was a dream. All of it. Turning hopeful eyes back to my husband, I ask, "Is Keelan doing well?"

Kallen frowns. "Do you not mean Kegan?" He stresses the G in his cousin's name. "And what would be wrong with my cousin that has you so concerned with his well-being first thing in the morning?"

Okay, so that really happened. I am still in a hell where Keelan doesn't exist and Kegan and Alita are not hand-fasted. Not wanting to push the topic any farther, I shake my head. "Nothing. Something bad happened to him in my dream. I'm still trying to shake it off." Biting my bottom lip, I try not to ask, fearing the answer, but I can't help myself. "Was there a tsunami yesterday?"

Kallen chuckles and pulls me back down next to him. "You do have vivid dreams. I certainly hope you dream of me on occasion. Me doing very naughty things with you."

I can't help but smile. "I don't need to dream about it. I have you in real life."

Giving me a delicious morning kiss, he grins against my lips. "Yes, you do. Perhaps we should practice some of those things right now."

I should jump out of bed and try to figure out what is going on. There was a tsunami. I know there was. But, I can't seem to tear myself away from my gorgeous husband's passionate embrace. Not that I'm really trying. I meet his kisses with my own rising excitement until a good portion of the next hour slips by in a blur of delirious pleasure.

A loud scratching at the door eventually brings us screeching back to reality. Kallen groans and rolls onto his back. "You should teach the beast some manners if we must keep him."

"It's completely hopeless, I'm afraid. Let him in." I would use my magic to open the door, but I'm afraid I would exert too much and blow it off its hinges. "Come on in, Taz."

When the door pushes forward, it is not Taz who saunters in. It is Felix. On a leash. There is no one holding the other end, though. "Taz?" he grunts. "Who the hell is Taz, you twit brain? There is no Taz here."

There are two reasons my mouth opens and then snaps shut, and does this repeatedly, for a full thirty seconds. First, Felix is not lying. He doesn't even set off a flicker in my natural lie detecting ability. He has no idea who Taz even is. Second, he never, ever, speaks to me like this. He goes out of his way to be polite and kind in an effort to leave his awful past behind. "What is wrong with you?" I finally choke out.

A snarl curls the Tasmanian devil's lip. "Nothing a trip back to my universe wouldn't cure. Keeping me in this hell hole is crueler than any torture my master ever devised. At least she was honest about her desire to break me. You cover it up with niceties and ply me with food. I will never tell you her secrets. Ever."

Tabitha comes hurrying into the room. "Sorry, little beast got away from me when I was trying to feed him. He bit me and took off. I figured he would come up here to cause trouble." It is only now I notice the bandage wrapped around her finger with blood seeping through it.

"He bit you?" I repeat like an idiot.

"You seem to have trouble grasping the concept. Let me show you exactly what happened." Felix is bounding toward the bed, teeth gnashing. In a flash, he is slumped on the floor in a pitiful heap and whimpering. He hit a solid wall of magic that I was too stunned to create. Kallen did it.

"Take him back downstairs and this time, do not lose him," Kallen orders Tabitha. "We will be down in a minute."

The older Fairy nods. Edging closer to the beast, Tabitha grabs his leash and tugs not so gently on it until Felix is forced to his feet. She drags him from the room.

For the second time in a minute and a half I am left stunned. First, that Felix tried to attack us, and second, that Tabitha did as Kallen ordered her to do. He didn't ask her nicely, he told her to do something and she did it. Without once trying to smack him in the head. Though, she did give him a pretty nasty look before leaving the room. I am beginning to suspect that this day may be stranger than the last. Not only that, it seems my only ally in this strangeness is now missing. My heart clenches. I hope Taz is okay.

As if sensing the direction of my thoughts, Kallen asks, "Who is Taz?"

I shrug noncommittally. "Just another Familiar from my dream. Not sure really where the name came from," I lie. It's getting easier and I don't like that.

Kallen wraps his arms around me, kissing the top of my head. "Thank goodness it was just a dream. The last thing we need is another Familiar from an alternate universe being left in our care."

I feel the need to defend Felix. After all, my Felix has been nothing but loyal and kind. "He's not so bad."

Kallen makes a choking noise and stares down at me. "Just last night you were suggesting we have roasted leg of Tasmanian devil for dinner."

"I was?" I am less concerned about the fact that I may have made such a comment, I make them about Taz all the time, than I am that Kallen has memories of conversations that we've never had. That's plain disturbing.

Shaking his head, he smiles. "Your dream really has thrown you off."

Yes, let's go with that explanation. "It has."

"Breakfast will help. Tabitha should have it finished by now."

I glance at the clock on the wall and frown. It's about two hours after the time Tabitha would normally have breakfast done. Regardless, I let Kallen lead me from the room and down the stairs. As we pass through the large living room on the way to the kitchen, I notice little things here and there that are different. Several paintings which normally adorn the walls are gone. Some knick-knacks are missing, replaced by others. Just little things, but enough of them that it is unlikely it would have happened overnight.

Seated at the kitchen island counter, we find Dagda drinking coffee and going over some papers. I have a smile ready for him, but it fades when he lifts his eyes to us. They are so filled with malice it takes my breath away. "Finally deigned to get out of bed, I see."

"Good morning, Dagda," Kallen says casually as he heads to the coffee pot and pours himself a cup. His tone is casual, but there is ice buried in his words. It puts me on edge. Kallen pours another cup of coffee and hands it to me. Frowning, I take it but immediately set it on the counter. I much prefer juice first thing in the morning and so does he. Normally. The fact that we are suddenly out of sync is so disconcerting, I don't hear the conversation around me until there is a loud clearing of a throat. I turn to my biological father.

"Do I finally have your attention?" he snarls.

A vision of the future pops into my head. Not because I'm psychic. But because if he speaks to me in that tone again, I am going to use my magic to cover him in honey and then roll him around in the sand. If he's lucky, I won't leave him for the fire ants to devour. "Yes," I say between gritted teeth. "You do."

There is wariness in his eyes now, but Dagda pushes forward anyway. "You insist upon me coming here every morning to go over every decision I am to make for the day, yet every morning you insist upon making me wait. If you are so determined to make a mockery of me, why not simply take the crown for yourself? You essentially wear it behind closed doors already."

Um. Yup, just 'um'. I can't think of any other reaction which is appropriate at the moment.

"You will take care with the tone you use when addressing my wife," Kallen growls. He looks ready to kill the Fairy. I've seen this look on his face before, but this is the first time I believe he may actually do it.

Trying to clear the cobwebs spun out of complete and utter confusion taking over my brain, I shake my head. I need to go with the flow here. I need to try not to make too many waves until I figure out what is going on.

Obviously, I woke up in a drastically different world than I did yesterday, but I can handle it. It seems likely that my typical response would be snarkiness, so I go with it. "Did Tana kick you out of the wrong side of the bed this morning?"

Dagda's face turns a shade of red akin to that of a clown's bulbous nose. "It is none of your business who shares my bed. However, I do not know this Tana you mention."

He doesn't know Tana? How can that be? Ah, it's starting to make sense. That's why Taz isn't here. Tana created Taz as a twisted sort of revenge that ultimately backfired since having a Familiar can actually be useful at times. Not many times, but there are times. If she and Dagda never met and married, he wouldn't have cheated on her when he seduced my mom and Tana would not have had reason to create a Familiar for me. Hence, no Taz in this strange world. My heart aches for the loss of him. I need to figure this all out so I can get the foulmouthed little beast back where he belongs. With me. Whether he is a pain in the butt or not most of the time, he is still one of my closest friends. Obviously, things are not this screwed up in the alternate universe if Felix was still created. How strange to think that universe is currently more normal than mine.

I wave my hand in the air as if it doesn't matter. "Just a maid I saw you ogling," I lie. Kallen gives me a strange look but lets the comment go. He knows I'm lying and he has no idea why, but he won't call me out on it in front of Dagda.

There is a loud and annoyed sigh behind me. I turn to find Mom floating in the doorway. "Xandra, you promised *he* would not be here this late anymore. I have the right to roam the house freely and not have to worry about running into him."

I want to cry. I want to rage at the cosmos. I can't believe it. Mom is a spirit again. Which makes sense, I guess. Tana was the one who figured out that Mom and Dad's bodies were still alive and well. If I end up stuck in this particular world, I am going to make sure I miraculously come to the same conclusion so I can fix this. For now, I need to address her concerns as she looks about to explode. Her making a scene will not help my current stress levels. "He's leaving soon, Mom," I promise even though I have no idea how long Kallen and I usually meet with the King. He could be here for hours yet.

Thinking of the King, I really hope I don't end up stuck in this world. I like the relationship I have with Dagda in my world. I don't want to boss him around, and I certainly don't want us to go back to hating each other. Considering the malice and contempt in his eyes as he stares at me, I seriously doubt there will be any chance of fixing it, though. That is some deep hatred he is harboring for me. I wonder what I did, besides being born, to deserve it.

"See to it that he does," Mom sniffs and floats back out of the kitchen.

"I will find a way to exorcise her," Dagda mutters under his breath.

Nope, no chance whatsoever of us fixing the rift between us in this world. "How long has it been since I tossed you through a wall?" I ask sweetly.

Kallen chuckles behind me, but says, "We should get down to business. Hand them over." He indicates the pile of papers in front of Dagda. For the next fifteen minutes, my husband and I go through them, vetoing this, agreeing to that, making notes on other things. Actually, Kallen does this. I simply agree since I have no idea what is going on in this realm currently, so I don't really have an opinion. Considering how it goes unnoticed, I can't help but wonder if I am this little help every day in their world. That's discouraging for my future as Queen in my own world.

When we are finished, Kallen dismisses Dagda. Handing him the papers back, he growls, "Leave."

My eyes widen in shock. Obviously, there is no love lost between them, but Kallen is never so gruff. Or rude. That's my job. After Dagda gathers the papers and shuffles out the door, I turn to my husband. "You were kind of mean to him."

Kallen's brows shoot to the top of his forehead and for a second, he looks like he had really bad plastic surgery. "The Fairy tried to kill you, again, not three nights ago."

Oh. That explains a lot. "I guess he deserved it then," I admit sheepishly.

Cocking his head, Kallen assesses me. "You have been behaving oddly since we rose. Are you unwell?"

I'm beginning to think I am. Since I will not be saying that out loud, I go with, "I think I just need some fresh air. Maybe a walk on the beach."

"I will come with you." Good to know he is considerate toward me in every world. It makes me smile.

Still, I shake my head. "No, I just need a minute alone to clear my head." And think about how I am going to stop this awful world jumping I am doing.

After another moment of studying me, Kallen finally nods. "Alright, but if you do not return soon, I will come looking for you. Dagda is likely to have Fairies on the lookout just waiting to catch you alone."

More curious than afraid, I ask, "Do they have a chance against me?" Maybe I'm weaker in this world.

Kallen snorts. "No one has a chance against you, my love." He pulls me into his arm and kisses me, making my heart glow. That glow is instantly doused by his next words. Pulling back, he says, "But the last Fairy who tried to assassinate you is still in a coma. I fear you will not be able to keep to your 'no killing' policy as the attacks grow in intensity."

I gulp audibly. "Oh."

His brow scrunching together, Kallen asks, "Had you forgotten?"

My eyes wide and round as Jupiter, I step back. "What? Forgot that I almost killed someone? No, of course not." I back away from him. "Um, I'm going for that walk now. I'll be back soon." I turn and hurry from the room before he can argue.

Behind me, I hear Kallen say to someone, "Follow her. Make sure she is okay." The true concern for my wellbeing in his voice more than makes up for him instructing someone to tail me. Who could it be, though? The only other Fairy I've seen was Tabitha. Surely she wouldn't agree to something like that. The Tabitha I know would tell him what he could do with the whole idea. Then again, the Tabitha I know doesn't exist here. Despite my curiosity over the matter, I don't stop to find out. My need for fresh air is growing exponentially.

Mom is floating back and forth in the large living room and I groan aloud. She is waiting for me. With a stern lecture, no doubt, about Dagda being here too long this morning. A lecture I have no intention of listening to at the moment. "I'm going for a walk," I say as I hurry past her.

Knowing a blow off when she hears one, she says, "I will accompany you."

"No, I want to be alone," I say in a tone which I hope will convey this is not up for debate.

"Xandra! Do not speak to me in such a way!" I guess my tone was not impressive, just irritating.

I try again. Narrowing my eyes, I take on the haughtiness Kallen had in his voice when addressing Dagda earlier. "I am going for a walk alone. We can talk when I get back."

This time, she understands that I mean it. Taken aback by my rebuff, Mom huffs, "We certainly will." But, she floats off in the opposite direction of the terrace doors. Thank goodness.

I step outside into the hot and blinding sun. I didn't realize the morning was so warm already. Shielding my eyes, I look up and down the beach deciding which way to go. Remembering the path I took when I came across the talking crab, I decide to go the opposite way. Not that I think I'd run into the crab again, but the fewer things which make me think I'm crazy the better. I won't go as far as Alita's cottage, though. I still can't face her knowing that Keelan is missing. I need to figure this out so Alita can have her son with her. And her husband.

It is Tabitha following me. I can sense her. She keeps a good distance between us and stays close to the tree line. I doubt it is so she can hide if I turn around. I suspect she is searching the forest for signs of Dagda's men. I find it both sweet and insulting at the same time. If there is someone lurking in the trees, I am just as likely to sense it as she is, and I've proven on many occasions that I can take care of myself. Even in this world, apparently.

After that little speech in my head, I feel rather embarrassed when the flapping of wings near my head makes me jump. I swat at the bird flying too close. "Get away from me!"

"The girl has spirit and is long of arm, but to me she will cause no harm. Adroit and swift of wing, to the air I will cling while dazzling you with this bird's many charms."

Sighing loudly, I shake my head. "Not another rhyming creature. This really is a special kind of hell I've found myself in."

8 Chapter

"Talking to yourself?" Tabitha calls from behind me. At least she knows she's not being stealthy. She was just trying to give me some privacy.

Still, I don't need a babysitter. I turn toward her. "You don't need to follow me. I'm fine."

"That last attack was a nasty one. Cannot hurt to have an ally close by if it happens again."

I wish I could ask more about the attack. It must have been nasty if Kallen is so worried about me being out here alone. Tabitha would probably think it odd if I asked about it, though, since I was actually there when it happened. And I won. At least, a version of me was there and won.

"Sun sure is bright today," Tabitha remarks, shielding her eyes. "Seems to be growing brighter by the second."

Now that she mentions it, I realize it's true. It is so bright, the light reflecting off the sand is actually hurting my eyes. My retinas are being permanently damaged, I'm certain of it. Shielding my own eyes, I point them toward the heavens. The sun is huge in the sky. I've never seen it appear so large. And it seems to be on fire. What the hell?

It doesn't take me long to figure out that the sun is not on fire. Because that's not the sun. Unless the sun is falling to earth at a gazillion miles per hour. Nope, that is something else entirely.

"Xandra!!" Kallen's shout reaches me over the sound of the growing waves. He is barreling toward us. I have never seen him run so fast.

Grabbing Tabitha's hand as I pass, I drag her along with me to meet him. When we are close enough, I shout, "I know. I see it!" He came to warn us. A lot of good that will do, unfortunately.

Engulfing me in his arms, Kallen crushes his lips to mine. "I love you," he manages after a minute. "For eternity."

"I love you, too." I press my lips to his again. I know I should try to stop it. I know I should be working a spell.

But, I couldn't stop a tsunami. The likelihood of me stopping a meteor the size of the sun falling to earth is too inconsequential to even think about. Okay, it's probably not the size of the sun. But, I've seen enough disaster movies over the years to know that a meteor this size is going to wipe out the entire planet. Or, at least, our portion of it.

So, I am not going to waste my time on a spell. I am going to kiss my husband for the final few seconds we have before everything is gone.

9 Chapter

The feel of Kallen's legs tangled with mine is so delicious, I can't help but snuggle closer and press my lips to his smooth skin even before opening my eyes. My hands wander over his muscled body, my arousal growing with every touch. I will never tire of touching him, of waking up next to him. He is forever mine.

Turning toward me, Kallen purrs softly, "Good morning, my love." He kisses me with a promise as to how good the morning is about to become.

When I do finally open my eyes, Kallen is the only thing I see. I am so wrapped up in the pleasure of being with him, making love to him, no other thought penetrates my mind. It is only after that thoughts finally begin to creep in. Meteors, Dagda, talking birds. I can't help a soft groan, but it is not in pleasure this time.

"What is it?" Kallen asks with a furrowed brow. He is holding my naked body close to his and is tracing invisible circles on my back. This usually calms me, but not now.

"What do you remember of yesterday?" I ask.

With a confused chuckle, he says, "I remember all of yesterday. Why do you ask such an odd question?"

"Did anything peculiar happen?"

"Are you referring to my cousin begging my grandmother to allow him to move in here on a permanent basis?"

Sure, let's go with that. Better than asking him if a giant meteor fell from the sky. Obviously it didn't as we are still here. "How do you think his father will take it?" I ask, assuming Kegan's relationship with his father in this world is as bad as it is in mine. Why else would he be begging to move in here?

Kallen shrugs. "Poorly."

There is a loud pounding on the door. "I have been sent to remind you of breakfast," Kegan shouts through the door.

With a sigh, Kallen kisses the top of my head. "Here for five minutes and he is already the errand boy."

"I heard that!" Kegan growls through the wood.

"I intended for you to hear it," Kallen grins at the door. Nope, some things never change. Still, Kallen disentangles himself from me and rises from the bed. Is it possible for a world to exist in which I don't love watching him stretch naked in the morning? I don't think so.

A sexy smile plays on my lips. "Come back to bed."

He turns lust filled eyes to me, but to my utter disappointment says, "And bear the wrath of the Queen? I do not think so."

The Queen? So, Tana does exist in this world. And upon closer inspection, there does seem to be a real bit of fear lingering in Kallen's eyes. Oh man, is she evil again? With growing dread, I push back the covers and climb out of bed, mentally preparing myself for a fight. In the back of my mind, there is also a ray of hope that I will find Taz alive and well.

After we freshen up and dress, Kallen and I head downstairs. I turn my feet toward the kitchen, but Kallen tugs on my arm. "Breakfast with the King and Queen, remember." He pulls a confused me toward the formal dining room.

Seriously? The formal dining room for breakfast? I try hard not to roll my eyes. As soon as we step foot in the room, though, I regret not having done so. If I had, my eyes would have been diverted for a fraction of a second longer from the ghastly sight they are now witnessing. I'm ready for that meteor to hit now. Or the tsunami. That would work, too. Anything to make this world disappear.

I press my eyelids together, hoping to erase the sight before me. I pry one open. Nope. Didn't work. I consider grabbing one of the forks from the table and just gouging my eyes out completely. Yes, that's what I'll do. Or does one use a spoon to rid oneself of her eyes? I suppose it doesn't matter. Either way will be painful, and possibly the pain will be so intense it will cleanse my soul of the grotesque sight before me.

"Are you okay?" Kallen whispers.

"You do seem pale, darling. Are you unwell?" Dagda asks. Darling? I am so not his darling. Especially not right now.

I'm in a different world, I keep telling myself. The most insane one of them all, apparently. Forcing my mouth to form a word, because I cannot manage more than one, I finally choke out, "Fine." I sit. Actually, my knees buckle and I fall into a chair. Again, the tsunami or meteor can hit any time now.

"Are you certain? You look rather peaked," Mom says.

I can't really focus on her words, though. Not when she is speaking them through the mouth that was just attached to my biological father's. Oh my god. Dad. Dad must not exist in this world. And if Dad doesn't exist, Zac doesn't exist. That realization sends me into another tailspin. This one not of shock but sadness. I try to keep the tears that want to spring into my eyes at bay. I am losing the battle.

Kallen brushes a tear from my cheek. The worry in his eyes when he turns my face so I can see him is heart wrenching. "Xandra, what is it? What is the matter?"

Choking back the rest of my tears, I square my shoulders. "Um, nothing. I'm just kind of emotional this morning. Not sure why." That sounds lame, but it's the best I can come up with. Seeing that everyone is staring at me as if I have six heads and twelve arms, I decide I can't make it worse. "Hey, I know what would help. Mom, why don't you tell me about how you and Dagda came to be…" I glance down at her ring finger to be sure and gulp back a choking sound, "…married."

Nonplussed, Mom peers more closely at me. "Xandra, what is going on? And why are you referring to your father by his given name?"

Pasting a smile on my face, I shake my head. "Nothing, really. And I was just trying out the name. Thought it would be fun. Sorry. But I would love to hear the story. Again," I add, assuming that in this world I have already heard it. Probably more than once.

After a quick glance at Dagda, and him patting her arm affectionately which makes me want to vomit, Mom nods. "Alright, dear." A genuine smile forms on her lips. Obviously, she loves this story. Ugh. Maybe I don't want to hear it, after all. I suspect it will only add to my growing nausea. "As you know, your father was angry with the Witches." She turns an affectionate gaze back to him. "But, when he came to seduce me out of spite, he found me absolutely irresistible. Instead of seeking to make war with the Witches, he decided to make peace instead. He wooed me until he made me his. It didn't take long," she sighs happily. "We were married within a month. Nine months later, we had you."

"So, I grew up here?" The words are out of my mouth before I can stop them. I clamp a hand over my lips and pretend to cough. Hard. After my fake choking episode, I attempt to wipe the extremely confused expressions from their faces. "I don't know why that came out as a question," I mutter. "Of course I grew up here. Wouldn't have wanted to grow up anywhere else."

Kallen reaches over and takes my hand in his. "I, for one, have always been glad you grew up here." His smile is so sweet, I can't help but lean into him and give him a light kiss. Leaning to the side, he whispers in my ear, "I first wanted to marry you when we were eight, if you recall. But, you made me wait six more years for our first kiss."

I grew up loving Kallen. Now, that is a world I would have enjoyed. Except for the complete ick factor of my biological parents being together, of course. Then again, I'm certain there was no ick factor in this world. Not if it was the only thing I knew. My heart still aches for Dad and Zac, though. I won't give up on them. I need to find my way back to my world where Mom is happy with Dad and Dagda is happy with Tana and I have a wonderful little brother.

"You still look pale. Maybe you should go back to bed for a while," Mom insists. "We can do breakfast another time."

"We are postponing breakfast?" Isla says from the doorway. She is quick to hide it, but I don't miss the glee in her eyes. These breakfasts with Mom and Dagda are obviously not her thing, either. I wonder if she can sense there is something wrong with the whole idea of it? She is very intuitive. Glancing at her watch, she says, "I will head to the palace now, then. Might as well get an early start to things." She can't leave the room fast enough. If only she took me with her.

Kallen rises from his chair and holds his hand out to me. "Come on, I will tuck you back into bed."

Hmm, stay and watch Mom and Dagda make googly eyes at each other or join Kallen in our room. I glance at my parents and shudder. Decision made. "Maybe a nap would help. I'm probably just coming down with a cold or something."

"Feel better, dear," Mom says, her forehead wrinkled in worry.

"Let me know if you are not going to make it to the palace this afternoon," Dagda says. "If we need to postpone the meeting with the Minister of Finance, so be it." I sit in on his meetings with the Minister of Finance? I guess I'm more involved with the running of the government in this world. Makes sense if I grew up around it. I probably understand everything about Fairy society and its laws in this world.

Since I am not from this world, going to that meeting would probably make me appear more of an idiot than I do right now. "Um, let's meet with him tomorrow," I suggest. With how things have been going, there probably won't be a tomorrow for me in this world. Unless I just jinxed myself and am now stuck here. I really hope not.

Wanting to make my escape, I hurry from the room with Kallen in tow. Walking hand in hand to the stairs, my steps slow and I actually find myself growing more curious about this world I find myself in. Of the three I've experienced now, I must say, this one is the most interesting. I grew up loving Kallen. My biological parents found love together. Life would have been much simpler if this was how it really happened.

"Why do we live here instead of the palace again?" I blurt out. I groan internally. I need to stop asking stupid questions.

To my surprise, Kallen chuckles. "I assume you are being facetious."

I roll my eyes. "Of course."

With a wry smile, Kallen says, "It is unfortunate our year respite is almost up. Soon, we will be back there."

So, we did live at the palace. We must have begged for the peace and quiet of Isla's mansion. A part of me is surprised Dagda agreed. Even in my world, he wants Kallen and me to live at the palace. He makes that suggestion rather frequently. We choose to ignore it just as frequently.

"Breakfast over so soon?" Kegan remarks from the terrace as we walk by.

We stop in the doorway. "Why weren't you there?"

Kegan snorts. "And watch your parents fawn all over each other. I would not have been able to keep my food down."

I can't help but defend them even if I was also a bit grossed out by their affection for each other. Okay, more than a bit. Lots more. "They're still in love after all these years. Leave them alone."

Kegan quirks a brow. "Someone is touchy this morning."

I give him a sheepish smile. "Sorry, I guess I'm a little under the weather."

"Come, we should get you back to bed," Kallen says, tugging on my hand.

I scowl at him. "You know I hate it when you order me around like a dog."

The sheer surprise on his face is enough for me to know that I'm not quite so sensitive about it in this world. How strange. "Like a dog?" Kallen repeats.

I can't help it; I roll my eyes. "Come. That's what you say to dogs."

"She really is touchy this morning," Kegan smirks.

"Say it again and I'll show you how touchy I am this morning," I grumble.

"Your grammar is suffering considerably, as well," Kegan pushes. "Why all the contractions?"

I scowl and open my mouth to say something about where he can put his opinion regarding my use of contractions when I realize he's right. If I grew up here, I wouldn't speak with contractions. Every once in a while a Fairy will let one slip, but for the most part, they consider it rude. I clamp my mouth shut again before I say something incriminating.

A wide grin breaks out on Kegan's face. "I have rendered you speechless. I do not believe that has ever happened before."

I glower at him. "We were on our way upstairs." I turn toward the terrace door and walk through it. I hear Kegan chuckling behind me. The chuckling stops after a soft thud of flesh meeting flesh. I believe Kallen just punched him in the arm. It is comforting to know some things don't change. I smile to myself as I walk up the stairs.

10 CHAPTER

In our room, I find the four walls confining. I need some air. I walk out onto the balcony and gaze at the ocean stretching out to the horizon. It's a calm, pleasant day here on the beach. No crashing waves or any other indication of a deep ocean volcano erupting. The sky is bright, not meteor crashing to the earth bright, just a nice, sunny day.

Hands slide around my waist and I sigh contentedly. It doesn't matter what world I'm in, Kallen's touch is a constant wonder. My skin tingles in the most delightful way. But, as always happens when I find a place of contented bliss, an ugly thought creeps into my head. This Kallen is different than yesterday's Kallen who was different than Kallen from the day before that. Oh my god. Am I cheating on my husband? With my husband? I groan aloud and slouch forward out of his arms. I'm tempted to jump off the balcony and run screaming into the sea. Things just keep getting worse, don't they?

"Xandra?" Kallen reaches for me again but I slip out of his reach. Frowning with concern, he asks, "What is wrong?"

"Oh, nothing a good meteorite crashing to the earth wouldn't cure," I grumble under my breath.

Growing irritated by my bad attitude, he says, "You are truly unwell. I am going to find Tabitha. Maybe she can give me answers." He is annoyed with me but I am fairly oblivious to it. I just figured out that I might be cheating on him with him, after all. That would make anyone a bit distracted.

"Okay." I wave him off, already absorbed in my convoluted thought process. He hesitates, but leaves me on the balcony alone after a moment. I'm relieved. I need to think this through.

So, in each day, I am still myself. Other than my behavior, no one thinks it's odd that I'm here. There isn't another me, so I'm not jumping universes. At least, I don't think so. I keep referring to these as different worlds, but I don't think that's accurate. In my gut, I feel confident that I am in my universe, my world, but my world is changing. The people are the same, at least physically, but their memories have been altered and their personalities either slightly, or like yesterday and Dagda, radically different. How is that possible? What is causing the changes?

The past. In each of the three different, for lack of a better description at the moment, worlds, a key event in the past has changed. Well, not changed, exactly. It didn't happen. Something important didn't happen. Why? Are the Angels trying to teach me a lesson of some sort? Am I supposed to be gleaning knowledge from this experience which I will carry with me into the future? Am I supposed to take the world ending disasters as a sign of things to come? Or are they metaphors, signs of my potential weaknesses? Thanks for that, if it's the latter, my dear Angel friends. Nothing like making someone feel inferior and weak when teaching them a lesson.

That doesn't feel right, though. It doesn't feel like a lesson. It feels more like I'm being taunted. Like someone is saying, look at how easily I can change your world. Then kill you with a freak natural disaster which no amount of magic could stop. Who would be that powerful? More importantly, who would want to torture me like that?

Back to my little Kallen issue. If past events are changing, but the people in my life are staying the same, I'm not cheating if I make love to my husband, right? I mean, he's still the same person. It's just his life experiences have changed. But physically. Physically, he is still my Kallen. And emotionally, he still loves me in each scenario. But, then again, I'm not necessarily the Xandra he really knows in each scenario, am I? Maybe I'm not cheating on him, but I'm forcing him to cheat on me. Or, at least, the me he knows. With the me he doesn't know. Lord, my head hurts.

"Fear and doubt cloud the brain, as realities weave in and out of this plane. Like the sway of spider's silk, time can be used to bilk, also used to control and constrain."

"Um, who said that?" I ask, searching for whatever creature has the power of voice and rhyme this time. I scan the balcony but I don't see anything. Great, is the air talking to me now?

"Xandra," Kallen says slowly from behind me. "Did that spider just speak to you? In rhyme?"

I whip around to where his eyes are glued to a spot above the balcony doors. There, in the corner, is an ugly black spider. It's only about an inch long, but what it lacks in size, it more than makes up for in presence. I take an unconscious step backwards. "Yup, it sure did," I confirm to Kallen. Nonplussed, I add, "I thought you were going for Tabitha."

"I decided I was overreacting," he says, taking a step closer to me. "Why is a spider speaking to you in verse?"

I shake my head. "I wish I knew."

"It sounded as if it was making a threat of some sort."

I consider this. "It did, didn't it?" As I play the words over in my brain, though, I change my mind. "Or warning me."

Kallen drags his eyes from the spider to meet mine. "Warning you about what?"

I make a decision. If this is really my Kallen, I need to trust him with what is going on and hope that he doesn't still think I'm crazy after I tell him everything. "We need to talk."

He stares at me long and hard then shakes his head. "This cannot possibly be good," he mutters. But, he holds a hand out to me and I take it. We edge past the spider and make our way back into our bedroom. He uses magic to close the balcony door. Hopefully, that will keep the spider on the outside of the house. I'm not in the mood to listen to any more stupid rhymes from creatures which shouldn't be able to speak at all.

Once we reach the bed, Kallen drops my hand and climbs on. He leans against the headboard and pats the spot next to him. "Come tell me what disaster has struck this time," he says with a wry smile. Yes, he is definitely my Kallen.

I sit next to him and take a deep breath. Letting it out slowly, I square my shoulders and force myself to tell him everything. He remains silent as the words spill from my mouth. When I am finished, I brace myself for his doubt, and the likelihood that he will want to have my brain examined. I watch him as he ponders everything I have said, rolling the words around in his mind. When he opens his mouth, I fear the words which will come out so much, I almost tell him I was just kidding and to forget everything I said. I bite my tongue hard enough to draw blood to keep from doing it.

Without a trace of accusation or doubt in his voice, Kallen says, "That would certainly explain why my memories are all so vague. And why I constantly feel as if the world is off somehow."

I blink for several long seconds. My mouth drops open for several more long seconds. For another several long seconds I seriously consider strangling the love of my life. "What?"

Kallen shrugs uncomfortably. "For the longest time, I have had the feeling something is not right in our world."

My eyes are wide as watermelons. "You never thought that, perhaps, you should share this information with me?"

Another uncomfortable shrug. "You seemed happy. I did not want my anxiety to spoil your happiness."

Dread laces my next question. "Only I was happy?"

His brow creases as he considers my question. I see the moment the meaning of it sinks in. Reaching out, he gathers me to him. "Oh god, that is not what I meant at all," he assures me. Pressing his lips to mine, he kisses me long and hard until I am absolutely breathless. Pulling back, he puts his hands on my cheeks and meets my eyes with fierce determination. He wants me to believe his next words. "There has never been a time I doubted our love or the pure, unadulterated happiness and joy I find in being with you. The rest of the world, my love, it was all about the rest of the world. The only thing that has felt right is you. But you seemed happy with the rest of the world and if you were happy, I was not going to try to change a thing."

A grin spreads across my face and I must kiss him again. He has no idea how much I needed to hear that. I kiss him yet again. Passionately. Before things get too carried away, I force myself to pull back. We have a lot to work through yet. "You really don't think I'm crazy?"

With a wink, Kallen says, "I believe I understand your extensive use of contractions now."

I roll my eyes at his grammar police response. "Yes, I know. It's a living in the Cowan realm most of my life thing."

He shakes his head in wonder. "We did not grow up together."

"Nope. You didn't even like me when we first met."

"I find that hard to believe," he scoffs.

"It's true." Thinking back to our uncomfortable breakfast, I add, "And seeing Dagda and my mom together really freaks me out. They hate each other. In my world, he seduced her and dumped her. Then tried to kill me."

Cocking his head to the side, Kallen asks, "Is it not pleasanter to live in a world in which that is not the case?"

I consider for a moment then shake my head. "No. In the real world, they are both happily married to other people. They are also on their way toward getting along now. And Dagda and I made our peace." Biting my bottom lip, I ask, "Do you think we should tell anyone else about this?"

Kallen is quick to shoot the idea down. "You said no one believed you when you tried before."

"Well, you didn't believe me, either, but you do now."

With a sexy wink, he purrs, "You have special ways of convincing me."

I roll my eyes but laugh. "I didn't use those special ways to convince you."

"True, but I believe it is still different for us. Our bond, our love, brings us closer together." He reaches out and plays with a strand of my hair, rubbing it between his fingers. "We are connected in a way we are not with the others in our life."

I understand what he means. "Our shared destiny."

Kallen nods. "Whatever is going on, I believe it is our shared destiny which keeps us from being pulled too far apart. It is also what helps us find our way back to each other."

I know he's right. Even the first day when everyone else was convinced I was, he claimed he did not think I was crazy. He believed there was something going on that we hadn't figured out yet. "Okay, we keep it to ourselves."

A scowl dips his brow and he jumps topics. "I am trying to figure out how a crab, a bird and a spider could speak to you."

"Skin Walkers?" I ask. I would have sensed if they were Fairies in their animal forms. So would he.

"No. Just like Fairies, Skin Walkers cannot speak in their animal forms. Nor do they have the power to alter realities."

"Who does have the power to alter realities."

"The Angels are the only beings I know can do such a thing." From the tone of his voice, it is fortunate there is not an Angel in the room currently. Kallen may not have the power of the Angels, but his growing anger could help make up for that. Come to think of it, I haven't seen Raziel or Adriel in any of these worlds. Why is that?

Still, I am quick to disagree. "I don't think it's the Angels."

"How can you be so certain?"

How can I be certain? "It just doesn't feel like it's them." Okay, that was lame. I try again. "Why would they do this? They've already told me that my life could have been different." I give him a sheepish look. Different because I could have chosen Raziel instead of Kallen. Moving on. "Why would they want to show me little differences? Plus, Angels aren't supposed to manipulate things like this. Everything that happened in the real world," at the moment I am assuming my world is the real world, "happened because of freewill. Changing things just for the sake of changing them takes away that freewill."

"You do have a point," Kallen admits but I hear the disappointment in his voice. It would have been so easy to blame the Angels. Not that we could have made them fix things, but it would have been a positive step toward figuring out what is going on.

"Unless it is a rogue Angel." Not certain how many shared memories Kallen and I still have, I ask, "Do you know who Belial is?"

"Psychotic Angel who has tried to kill my wife on several occasions? I may have heard of him," Kallen says dryly.

I give him another sheepish look. "Sorry, I don't know what events occurred in both the reality I know and the one you now remember."

Sighing, Kallen nods. "You are right, of course. You do need to clarify these things."

"Anyway, do you think he could be behind this?"

Kallen shakes his head adamantly, but stops suddenly. "In your reality was he carted off and stripped of his wings?"

"Yes."

He goes back to shaking his head adamantly. "Then no, it is not possible."

"He had friends," I push.

Raising a skeptical brow, Kallen asks, "Friends willing to end up with the same fate?"

"Probably not."

"Have you pissed off any other Angels in your reality?"

I give him my best glare. "No," I huff. But, I do take a second to think about it. Have I? Not that I can think of, but I do tend to piss other beings off on a regular basis. It's hard to keep track.

"Nor have you in this one. At least, not to the degree necessary to make someone want to change your entire world."

"Glad to hear it," I mutter.

Kallen chuckles. "Would you rather I pretend you are tactful and demure in this reality?"

"Lord no," I scoff. "I seriously doubt my own personality could change that much." Now that I think about it, no one's personality changed that much. Not really. Not even Dagda's. What I saw of him yesterday was probably what everyone in the Fae realm saw when he was angry with the Witches and wanted me dead. In yesterday's reality, he never got over it like he did in mine. I just never personally experienced him being like that. I share this theory with Kallen.

He's not one hundred percent convinced, but mostly because his perception has been skewed by this reality. "It is difficult to imagine the King that way." I notice he says King, not uncle. Because in this reality, his mother's sister never married Dagda. He's not related to the King by marriage. Well, he is. Through me. So, Dagda is not his uncle by marriage anymore. "Still, if that is the case, it is useful information. Whoever is doing this can alter the realities, but not the beings themselves."

"What about the natural disasters?" I ask abruptly, my mind jumping topics on a whim.

Pursing his lips, Kallen says, "I believe those must have been imagined."

I glower in his direction. "Are you calling me crazy again?"

With a grin, he says, "Not any crazier than you normally are."

"That was not a compliment, nor did it make me feel better."

Leaning forward, Kallen kisses me softly. "Better?" he asks.

I smile. "Yes. Wait, no. What did you mean?"

"About you being crazy or about the natural disasters?"

I roll my eyes. "The disasters. I know I'm not crazy." As much as a person shifting realities can know such a thing.

"They marked the end of a reality, right?"

"Yes."

"Perhaps it was a way to reset the day."

"Destroying the world is one hell of a way to reset a day," I argue.

Kallen glances around the room. "I do not believe the world was ever actually destroyed."

He does have a point. I reluctantly acknowledge it. "I suppose you're right."

This elicits a soft chuckle. "Please, try to sound less excited about it."

"But to make me think that a world has ended? To fake a natural disaster? That takes a lot of magic. What about gods and demigods like Zeus or the Apsaras? They probably have the power to make it appear as if the world is ending."

Kallen looks at me askance. "Why would Zeus take an interest in our life?"

I open my mouth to make a snarky remark reminding him of how Zeus recently hit on me, when I snap it closed again. Kallen has no idea I know Zeus. That *he* knows Zeus. Because we met him through Hades who we met through Tana. Tana isn't in this reality, or, at least, not in the capacity of betrayed wife, so she never went to Hades and Kallen and I never went to the underworld to rat him out to his wife.

"Xandra, what are you not telling me?" I close my eyes, hoping if I can't see him, he can't see me. "Xandra? You know I can see you, right?"

Hmm, guess I've tried this before in this reality. Opening my eyes again, I say, "It's a long story. Suffice it to say, we know Zeus. Though, he seems to like me well enough, so I doubt it was him."

It's the blush which gives me away. "He likes you? How much does he like you?"

"Um, enough that I had to drag you away before you punched him."

To my surprise, Kallen grins. "Good to know I am not a coward in your reality."

I roll my eyes. "Being jealous of a god does not make you brave." Narrowing my eyes, I add, "And it's our reality, not just mine."

Shifting uncomfortably, he admits, "I am not quite used to the idea as of yet."

I can't blame him. Reaching over, I cup his cheek with my palm. "Any reality we are in together is our reality." I lean forward and kiss him lightly.

Before the kiss has a chance to carry us away, a thought slams into my brain. "Oh my god, the spider!" I practically shout. I scramble off the bed and start pacing. "With the crab there was a tsunami. With the bird there was a meteorite." I whirl to face Kallen. "What kind of natural disaster can be associated with a spider?" The world is going to end again soon. How can we stop it? I do not relish the idea of waking up to a new reality and having to convince Kallen all over again that the realities are shifting.

For the first time since we began, Kallen looks at me as if I may truly be insane. "I do not follow."

I let out a frustrated sigh. "Crab, water. Bird, sky. The rhyming creatures were precursors to a natural disaster. Since the spider talked to me, a disaster is coming. Soon. So, what kind of disaster could a spider be associated with?"

I watch the wheels in his brain spin. Emotions play over his face so clearly, I can see each step of his thinking process. Unusual as Kallen is generally good at poker faces. So, this is a treat. It starts with believing his wife insane and passes to light disbelief to 'it could be possible' to 'shit, she's right.' I would feel more gratified when he gets to the last one if it wasn't for one, it took so long, and two, this reality is going to reset.

Kallen starts listing possibilities. "Earth? They live in dark, dank places. Maybe an earthquake? Spiders spin webs, so possibly a tornado of great magnitude?"

I grimace. "Either of those would suck."

Cocking a brow, my charming husband asks, "Suck worse than a tsunami or a meteorite falling from the sky?"

Just because he has a point does not mean I need to be gracious in accepting the fact. "Right now, you suck," I grumble under my breath.

Eyebrow still cocked, Kallen does his own grumbling. "Switching realities makes you rather mean spirited."

Okay, that shames me. "Sorry." It's a one-word apology, but it's heartfelt.

Kallen realizes this because he leans forward and kisses me. "Apology accepted."

"So, back to the spider. We should be on the lookout for an earthquake or a tornado. Which one do you think would be more likely to kill us all?"

"Hard to say. Either can be devastating on a grand scale."

As if we asked for it, the wind begins to beat against the windows. It quickly picks up speed and is soon pounding against the walls of the mansion like a thousand battering rams. The sound is deafening. The walls begin to creak and shake, the house rocking on its foundation. Tornado it is then.

"We should try to stop it!" Kallen calls above the crashing wind.

"It's no use!" I call back. I really hate to sound so defeatist, but I have been through this a couple of times already. Besides, he is the one who first taught me long ago on a mountain in Colorado that magic is no match for natural disasters. Not to mention, we know that this isn't going to actually kill us. Just change the reality. I hope. I really, really, hope.

Reaching for me as the walls begin to tear apart, Kallen presses his lips to mine and he kisses me like this will be our last kiss ever. I kiss him back, matching his passion with my own. We are still caught in our embrace when the ceiling collapses upon us and the world goes black.

11 CHAPTER

My eyes open to the streaming sun again. Kallen is curled around me and I snuggle into the warmth of his gorgeous body. His arms tighten around me and he growls low in his throat before pressing his lips to a very sensitive spot behind my ear. He kisses a trail along my jaw until he reaches my lips. After a long, deep kiss, he murmurs, "That was one hell of a storm."

Shocked, I practically knock him out with my elbow in my haste to sit up. "What did you say?"

Pressing a hand against the eye which will probably turn black and blue if I don't heal it soon, Kallen sits up, as well. "I said, that was one hell of a storm."

"You remember it?"

Understanding seeps into his expression and he drops his hand from his eye. Oh, that is definitely going to leave a mark. "I do."

"Does that mean we're in the same reality?" I glance around wildly as if I am going to find the answer to that question on the walls of our bedroom.

Throwing back the covers, Kallen rises, dressing as he goes. "We should find out."

I find myself not as eager as he is. "Must we? Maybe we can skip today. Hang out here and just wait for the disaster to hit." I'm not a coward, I'm just tired. This blacking out when the disasters hit isn't very restful. I feel like I haven't slept in days.

I get a scowl for my reluctance. "Or, we could figure out what is happening and stop it."

Sighing, I push the covers back. "Fine, if you're going to be all reasonable about it."

Kallen chuckles softly and comes around to my side of the bed. "I am." Pulling me off the bed, he holds me close. "After I kiss you senseless."

Wrapping my arms around his neck, I smile. "Much better." He proceeds to kiss me senseless which, I admit, does nothing to further my motivation to leave the room.

I have no choice, though, when he ends the kiss and steps back. "Ready?"

"Sure." I sound like I'm on my way to my own funeral with my utter lack of enthusiasm.

Trying to be encouraging, he says, "We could be back in our own reality." As soon as the words leave his mouth, he stops and stares at me with wide eyes.

"What?" I demand, suddenly very worried.

"I remember." He shakes his head as if to clear it. "I remember our reality." Bringing his eyes to mine, he continues. "Not the reality where you grew up in the Fae realm, but our reality. The one with your Dad and your brother and my aunt. The other reality is fading in my mind."

I am so happy to hear it, I throw my arms around him and kiss him again. When I let him up for air, I am grinning from ear to ear. Not literally. That would involve some lip stretching exercises I simply haven't done. "We must be back in our reality." I grab his hand and yank. "Come on, let's go see everyone!"

I pull him to the door and throw it open, not caring that it hits the wall. We take the stairs at a run. Even though I have seen almost everyone daily, I miss all of them terribly. The real them, not the creepy versions of them I have met these past few days.

I stop mid-step when I hit the living room. Literally. Not a wise thing to do. Actually, I didn't even know it was possible. Technically, it's not. I don't stop. Which is how I end up tripping and falling to my knees rather painfully.

Every last bit of furniture in the living room is covered in white linen. I've only seen this in movies. When a house is to be left without inhabitants for a long time, people cover the furniture to keep it from getting too dusty. But why was it done here when there are obviously enough people living here to keep things from getting dusty? Our room wasn't dusty, nor were there sheets covering everything. "What is going on?" I whisper more to myself than Kallen. Getting to my feet, I hurry from room to room with him on my heels. It's the same everywhere. White linens draped over every piece of furniture. The only room not like this was our bedroom.

In the kitchen, I pull open cupboard doors and check the pantry and fridge. Nothing. There is nothing in all of them. Not one bit of food. I turn wide, scared eyes to Kallen.

His expression is grim and he says the words I don't want to admit are true. "No one lives here."

I lift my hand to brush at a tear which is determined to form in my right eye, but stop with my arm hanging in the air. I tense as I feel the magic swell around us. Not natural disaster magic. Fairy magic. Kallen feels it, too. He comes forward and puts his hand in mine as we both draw our own magic, ready to repel whoever is coming. For the magic we feel is most definitely hostile.

The kitchen door slams open and a Fairy neither of us has seen in a very long time stomps through it. "Get your hand off my husband, you half-breed bitch."

Husband? I glance up at the Fairy who is most definitely my husband. I honestly don't know who is more horrified. Me or Kallen. Okay, it's probably a draw.

12 Chapter

"Excuse me?" Kallen finally chokes out.

Xenia steps farther into the kitchen, her hands fisted at her sides. "What, you thought you could run off to your exiled grandmother's house with your lover and I would not come looking for you? At least try to come up with someplace original for your rendezvous!" She begins pacing back and forth. "I am Queen, dammit! You will not continue to embarrass me this way!"

I glance up at Kallen and watch as his shock fades to disgust which combines neatly with anger. "I am not your husband," he growls.

This stops Xenia. "Not this argument again. You know as well as I do that the rite was binding."

A weight lifts from my chest. She's talking about the rite Kallen's mom and Xenia's mom performed when they were babies. Which means Kallen didn't actually go through a hand-fasting with Xenia in this reality. In fact, I am so relieved that I don't realize my mouth has opened and I am speaking about something else entirely. "But, I stopped you before you became Queen."

Xenia bursts out laughing. "Whatever are you talking about? You were not even in this realm when I became Queen. You simply kept me from accessing the Cowan realm." Her eyes take on a steely edge. "Something I will rectify soon enough."

Got it. I missed the coronation but saved my home realm when she tried to come through and take over. That's a relief. At least, it is until a ton of dread rains down on me. "Um, what happened to Dagda again?" I ask, trying hard to sound nonchalant. Since I am asking what is tantamount to a very stupid question in this reality, I am not surprised by the nasty, dumbfounded look I get from Xenia.

"You grow stupider over time. I did not believe it possible, but it is amazing the rate at which it occurs," she cackles.

Kallen sends his magic out, but mine reaches her first. I have her pressed against the wall and her neck firmly caught in a chokehold. "Watch it," I warn. I couldn't care less that she is Queen. This isn't my reality. And she will not insult me. Whatever Xenia sees in my eyes wipes the snide humor from hers. "Where is Dagda," I growl, no longer caring if I sound stupid or not.

I need to lessen the magic holding her throat closed so Xenia can respond. "He is where he has been since the revolution. Chained in iron in the cells," she rasps.

My heart is torn. Part of it is relieved. The other part is horrified. He is alive. But, a Fairy chained in iron? Dagda is probably on the brink of death and he is certainly in a great deal of pain. It makes me want to increase my magical hold on her throat again. Which I must do, subconsciously of course, because she is turning the most marvelous shade of blue. Quite the contrast to her dull green eyes.

"Xandra." Kallen places a hand on my shoulder. "As much as I would like you to finish what you have begun, she is the Queen."

I shrug. Like I care who she is in this reality. "So."

"Before we start a war with the entire Fairy population, we should probably learn more about our current situation."

With great, and I mean great as in Herculean, effort, I let Xenia go. My voice is low and hard when I speak. "Get out. Do not come back here or I will finish what I began. Even if that means killing every single Fairy who stands with you." I wouldn't really do it, but she doesn't know that.

"You would not," she wheezes through her effort to replenish her air supply. Okay, maybe she does know I wouldn't start killing off Fairies.

"I have convinced her it is the right thing to do," Kallen says with the wickedest smile I have ever seen grace his lips. "My hatred of you knows no bounds and Xandra is willing to stand with me until your death if need be to make things right in this realm. As a matter of fact, we were just discussing how ending you would end all of the trouble this realm currently faces." I know he's lying, but he's doing an excellent job of it. A part of me is beginning to believe him. Dragging my eyes from Kallen to Xenia, I see that his lie is working on her, as well. She believes every word he's saying. When her eyes shoot to me, I paste my best serene smile on my face. As if I am perfectly fine with the abrupt change in my personality and sudden willingness to actually commit murder.

Edging toward the door, Xenia growls, "You cannot stand against the entire Fairy army. I will find a way to rid my realm of you once and for all. Then I will go after those Cowans you hold so dear." She stomps outside to the small army she brought with her. Really glad she left them outside, but it's strange she did if she hoped to drag Kallen back to the palace. I wonder if it was to ease her embarrassment over him meeting a lover, or because she knew they were no match for me when she realized he wasn't alone. Probably both.

When they have left the property, Kallen slumps back against the kitchen counter. "Grandmother in exile and Dagda in chains. What a reality we have been dropped into."

I snort. "Now you feel my pain of the last few days."

He gives me a sheepish smile. "Yes, now I understand." He pulls me closer as his expression sobers. "I am very proud of you. You have bravely faced alone what each day has thrown at you."

Which brings us to a very salient point. "Why are you aware today? Why aren't I alone again?"

"I have been wondering the same thing. The only conclusion I can draw is that by making me consciously aware of what was going on, you somehow dragged me out of the loop." He pauses a moment then adds, "Or, it could simply be that we were kissing when the world ended last time."

I shake my head. "No, I don't think that's it. We were embracing when the meteor hit. I believe you were right the first time. It's because you were consciously aware of what is going on when the tornado killed us."

"Technically, it did not kill us," he points out.

I wave a hand at him. "Semantics. It killed that reality."

"I am not certain that was a correct use of the word semantics," Kallen insists. I just glower at him in response. Wisely changing the subject, he says thoughtfully, "You were not even upset by the fact that I may have been married to Xandra in this reality."

Okay, maybe he didn't *wisely* change the subject. "Did you want me to act like a jealous wife and demand a duel or something?" I ask sourly.

Startled, he shakes his head. "No, not at all. I was just making an observation. Though, I must admit, I would have been furious if you were married to someone else for whatever reason."

"Honestly? I didn't believe her."

Surprised, Kallen asks, "Why not? Stranger things have happened in previous realities."

With a smile, I stand on my toes to kiss him. "Because there is no reality where you could be married to her. Your personality could not alter that much."

Kallen grins. "No, it could never alter that much." He kisses me again before resting his forehead against mine. "Thank you for believing that," he says softly.

As much as I would like to stand here and continue to kiss my gorgeous husband, we have work to do. "So, do we round everyone up and make them believe us now?" I ask. We had decided not to try to convince anyone else as we search for a solution, but if it pulls them out of the changing reality loop, maybe we should.

Kallen shakes his head. "No, simply for the fact that it does nothing more than make them aware. My knowing did not change the fact that the realities shifted. We need to figure this out on our own."

Nonplussed, I ask, "Don't we want them to be more aware?"

With a worried grimace, he says, "Who knows how that will affect them. Do you really want Kegan and Alita to be aware that their child no longer exists?"

I hadn't thought about it like that. "That would make me insane." I'm going crazy knowing their child is gone. I can't imagine if it was my own.

"Precisely. Which is why we need to figure this out on our own," he reiterates.

"How?" I ask miserably. "Where do we even begin?"

A corner of Kallen's mouth props up. "With magic, of course."

I eye him speculatively. "What are you thinking?"

Wrapping his arms around me, he grins. "I am thinking the one with whom I am truly hand-fasted is one of the most powerful beings in the universe. Certainly she can come up with a spell which would give us a clue as to where to search."

Hey, what is that on my chest? Oh, yeah, a great big ball of unreasonable pressure to complete a monumental task. Good thing I'm used to the weight of those things. Otherwise, I might be crushed by it.

13 Chapter

"But, what am I casting the spell for?" I ask. "I need to be specific."

Kallen is quiet a moment as he considers my question. Funny, it's usually me who has to stop and consider such things as 'a spell needs to be specific.' Finally, he says, "We must be very careful. I fear that if you simply create a spell to keep the realities from changing, we will be trapped in this one."

My belly roils like I just ate spoiled oysters topped with moldy olives with a glass of lumpy, rancid milk to top it off. "A reality where Xenia is Queen, Isla is in exile and we have no idea where everyone else is. I don't think so. What's the next option?"

"You could reverse the magic causing the reality," he suggests.

I ponder this idea a moment before shaking my head. "Considering how many realities I've experienced, it might be tricky to reverse it back to the beginning. I would hate to get stuck somewhere else along the way."

Kallen nods. "Good point."

"Can't I cast a spell requiring the person performing the magic to present him or herself?"

"Exposure magic is rather tricky," Kallen begins. "It also requires a ritual." He glances around the empty kitchen. "I doubt we have the items necessary at our disposal."

I shrug. "I'm pretty good at winging it."

My gorgeous husband gives me a dubious look. "You are also good at blowing things up when you do that."

I wave him off. "I haven't blown anything up in a while."

His eyes narrow. "Just last month you wanted to drive the carriage." I gulp. This story is going to make me look bad. "You powered it with so much of your magic that instead of driving it, you ended up in a pile of shards in the driveway." Several of which stabbed me painfully in the butt.

"What do you suggest then?"

"We need access to the archives."

I quirk a brow. "*You* are suggesting that *I* go into the archives? You aren't afraid I'm going to somehow blow the realm into a million pieces like I did the carriage if I do?" I tease.

With a grin, he says, "If you do, it will reset."

"You hope," I counter, not liking the very real fear lurking in his eyes. He is afraid I might blow up the realm if I spend too much time in the archives. I would be insulted if it wasn't actually true.

His face suddenly sober, Kallen holds a finger to his lips. I feel it now, too. I hate to do it, but I draw magic. Kallen and I move to the corner of the room, waiting for the newcomer to step into the kitchen.

She rounds the corner and stands akimbo before us. She doesn't care a flying fig about our drawn magic. "Just what the hell do the two of you think you are doing? We discussed just two days ago how you were going to *not* rendezvous here anymore. Draws too much attention. Not to mention, you are a hair's breadth away from being hand-fasted the way you sneak off to be alone together."

I open my mouth to contradict her but snap it closed. My heart clenches at her words and I glance up at Kallen. We're not hand-fasted in this reality? Well, that bites horse butts. Kallen's expression goes blank, proving he is by far the better between the two of us at poker faces. I'm certain I look guilty as hell.

"Of course, we apologize. We should know better," my husband lies smoothly. We didn't know better before we were married in our reality, why would we be any different in this one?

Appeased somewhat, or she just knows us well enough even in this reality to know that is the best she is going to get from either of us on the matter, Tabitha changes the subject. "What were you saying about the archives?"

"We need a spell to identify someone casting a spell," I blurt out, earning me an exasperated glance from my husband. We did just agree to keep this between ourselves. Oops.

Suspicion filling her green eyes, Tabitha gives me a long, assessing look. "What kind of spell?" she finally asks.

Well, I'm already neck deep in 'I shouldn't have said that.' I might as well fill the tub further and see if I can still swim. Um, probably not the soundest logic I've ever thought in my head, but still, I'm going to tell her. At least, I'm going to tell her part of it.

"Someone is trying to mess with reality," I hedge. "We want to stop him. Or her." No reason to be sexist about it. Besides, I've discovered the hard way that men and women can be pretty darn equal when it comes to doing evil deeds.

"What do you mean, *mess with reality*?"

Kallen sighs and shakes his head. He has accepted the fact that there is no going back now. "Reality keeps shifting from day to day. We need to put an end to it so we can all get back to the reality we are supposed to be in."

Tabitha stares at us long and hard. The words 'you are bat shit crazy and I don't believe you' should be tattooed on her head at the moment. Since that is obviously what she is feeling. Tabitha has never been difficult to read emotion-wise.

Proving my point, she says, "Do you really expect me to believe that load of bull?"

Calm, cool and collected like I never am, Kallen says, "Yes."

Tabitha studies him a bit longer. More than a bit, actually. She studies him so long that I'm tempted to think of a spell which will make her speak. Just as the words are forming in my mind, she blurts out, "Is this other reality one in which Xenia is not Queen?"

Kallen's lips quirk but he doesn't grin yet. "Yes." Me, I'm smiling like a hyena.

Tabitha nods. "Then we will find a way to get you into the archives."

I don't think she really believes us. Not really. I think she is just so disgusted with how this reality is for her right now, she's willing to try anything to change it. I wonder where she lives if she doesn't live here. With Kegan or Alita, maybe? I'm not going to ask. She looks miserable enough as she glances longingly around the house. I'm not going to ask her a bunch of questions which will make her feel even worse. Maybe she's hoping that my magic will bring a new reality on instead of, as Kallen and I claim, fixing an old one. It doesn't really matter either way. She is willing to help us. Which is all that matters.

"Excellent," Kallen says, finally letting his grin unfold across his face.

Tabitha surprises us both when she says, "We will need to rescue Dagda."

"What? Why?" I ask. My face turns a brilliant shade of fuchsia when I realize how callous that sounded. "I mean, we can rescue him after going to the archives, can't we?" I want to hurry up and get the spell cast so this reality doesn't exist at all. Then Dagda won't even need saving because everything will go back to normal. I hope.

Glowering at my lack of empathy, Tabitha drawls, "Not if you want access to the archives. The scribe will only let the rightful monarch pass through the doors."

"Um, how does that work?" I ask. Xenia is a pretty powerful Fairy. It seems like she could easily bully her way into the archives if she so desired.

Tabitha is now looking at me as if I've grown two heads. One of them I suspect strongly resembles that of a baboon. Or a baboon's butt. "What is wrong with you?" she asks. She reaches out to feel my forehead.

Stepping back, I scowl at her hand. So annoying how people always assume I am ill in these realities. "Not my reality, remember?" I blurt out a bit harsher than I meant to do.

Pulling her hand back, Tabitha purses her lips and narrows her eyes. She opens her mouth and I expect a chastisement about lying or something like that, but instead, she says simply, "You gave him the spell."

Him? The scribe here is a him? I glance up at Kallen and he gives a little shake of the head. Don't ask more questions, it will only upset her his expression tells me. I do a great big snort inside my head. When has that ever stopped me? "The scribe is male?" I blurt out. I'm doing a lot of blurting in this conversation.

Brow folding into a deep frown, Tabitha says, "Yes, and he has been scribe since before I was born."

Ah. Tana must not be around to kill him in this reality. Or hasten his demise with a heart attack. Makes sense. I wave the subject away. "Of course. So, if I gave him the spell, why won't he open up the archives for me?"

"Because the last time he granted you access you destroyed a large section of ancient scrolls. You promised to never return." I open my mouth to ask how I did it, but close it again. It doesn't really matter. "Needless to say, he does not like you," Tabitha adds. Unnecessarily, I believe.

"Yes," I mutter, "It was needless to say that." This earns me a glare which I soundly ignore.

"How do we get to Dagda?" Kallen asks before Tabitha and I go at it. "Xenia said he is locked away."

"The same way we always get to him," Tabitha snaps. She is obviously losing patience with the 'other realities' thing.

"Look, I know you don't believe us, but can you at least pretend you do?" I ask. "Things will move along faster that way."

Sighing, Tabitha nods. "Kegan will let us pass."

"Kegan?" I gasp. "What does he have to do with this?" I glance up at Kallen. He is wondering the same thing.

Deciding it really is easier to assume that we don't know what is going on, Tabitha explains, "To prove his loyalty, his father arranged for Kegan to guard Dagda. Which is why we have not broken him out long before this. Kegan's wellbeing is tied to Dagda's continued imprisonment."

Kallen's eyes harden. "The Kegan I know is not too cowardly to try."

Tabitha's eyes harden to the same degree. "Neither is this Kegan. It is Dagda who refuses to put Kegan's life in danger. We have tried to rescue him but he refuses to have any of it. He will not come with us." She stares at me long enough for me to understand she is glaring accusingly, and then turns back to Kallen before continuing. Whatever she is going to say next is obviously my fault. "With the passages closed, where would he and Kegan hide if he escaped?" Yup, my fault.

Not liking the idea that I am responsible for my biological father's continued imprisonment, I insist, "I would protect them."

Tabitha snorts. "Protect a man you despise?"

"I don't despise him," I protest.

Hands on her hips, Tabitha laughs. There is not a trace of humor in it. "You could have decided that a while back. Things might have been different."

Oh. I guess I didn't come to Dagda's rescue even though I hated him in this reality like I did my own. Feeling sheepish, I admit, "Yeah, I probably should have."

Kallen wraps an arm around my waist and pulls me close. "Can you bring us to Dagda?"

Nodding, Tabitha says, "That is the easy part. Getting to the archives will be the tricky part."

"We must try," Kallen insists.

"Then let us go and get this over with. If there is even the slightest possibility of changing this reality, I would like to see it done sooner as opposed to later."

"Wouldn't we all," I concur.

14 Chapter

We make our way through the woods to the palace. Tabitha leads us around to the back and we sneak in through a side door. Considering how much magic the three of us are exuding, and the fact that Fairies would be able to sense it, I suspect the palace Fairies simply do not care that we are here. Considering the fact Xenia is their Queen, they probably do not care about much. Maybe they are hoping we have come to save them. Which we have, so it all works out. At least, I am hoping it will. Otherwise, this reality will end in a natural disaster and we will all die. Probably not the worst thing which could happen at this point.

Inside the palace, we quickly make our way to the cells. I skid to a halt when I see Kegan pacing back and forth before a door. He glances up in surprise when he feels us approaching. He blanches. "What are you doing here?" He's talking to me.

No sense in easing into this. We don't have time. There must be at least a few guards who are loyal to their Queen. If only because they don't want to lose their heads. "We came to get him out of here."

"Right," Kegan scoffs. Standing to his full height, he says, "I will not let you kill him. I understand he wronged you, but that is not the Fairy he truly is."

I roll my eyes. "I know that. And I am not going to kill him." Geez, what kind of reputation do I have in this reality?

Looking to Tabitha for confirmation, Kegan asks, "Is she telling the truth?"

Tabitha shrugs. "As best as I can tell."

"Thanks for the vote of confidence," I mutter.

Kegan's eyes shift to Kallen and Kallen gives him a slight nod of encouragement. After a long moment, Kegan decides to take their word for it. He opens the door behind him. As I walk past, he says softly, "I will be watching you."

I could point out to him that I could easily take away his vision so he could, in fact, not watch me, but I do not. No sense in putting him even more on edge than he already is. I do not want to hurt him if he decides to do something stupid.

Inside the room, I stop short. All thoughts of Kegan or anyone else flee from my mind. A Fairy I barely recognize is lying on a bare cement floor. His black, stringy hair is past his shoulders. He has a matted beard which is just as long. He is dressed, but barely. His clothes are in tatters, singed around the torn edges. This is from the reaction of iron burning Fairy skin. When we were told that Dagda was in iron, it was not an exaggeration. At least seven different bands of iron are circling various parts of his body. One on each arm and leg. One around his torso and another around his neck. The cruelest by far, though, is the one wrapped around his mouth. That makes my taking his voice away from time to time seem kind in comparison. Okay, not kind exactly, but certainly much less psychotic. I brush at my eyes, pushing the gathering tears away.

I didn't realize I was moving closer to the cell until Kallen's hand catches my arm. "I am certain there are alarms," he says softly.

Kegan confirms this. "If the glass is tampered with, it immediately alerts Xenia."

"The glass?" I repeat.

Kegan nods. "Yes. If anyone attempts to bring down the glass barrier, she will be instantly aware."

"Is anything else alarmed?" I ask, glancing around the small room hoping that I haven't already triggered something by mistake.

"There is no need," Kegan says with a shrug. "There is no way to rescue him without the removal of the glass."

I was hoping he would say that. I also hope all my powers work in this reality. Time to test it out. In a blink, I am on the other side of the glass. It turns out the glass is soundproof, because I can only see Kegan and Tabitha's reactions, not hear them. Kallen's lips curl up into a proud smile and he winks at me. He turns to his cousin and Tabitha and must explain my ability to teleport because they are gawking at me in wonder now.

My focus turns to the tortured Fairy before me. My heart breaks as I take in his damaged skin up close. He is burned to the bone around his wrists. I can't believe he hasn't died of infection. I can't stand the sight of it, but I refuse to close my eyes as I pull magic. If he is brave enough to endure this torture, then I can be brave enough to face him. After all, in this reality, it is partially my fault that he has ended up like this. It only takes a second to free him of the iron. I almost vomit when I see his face once the iron is removed from his mouth. His lips are completely gone. His teeth and gums are charred.

Pulling more magic, I must force myself to proceed slowly. I want him to be healed instantly, but I can't do that. Healing can hurt almost as much as the injury itself and the faster it happens, the worse it can be. I don't go too slowly, though. We don't have that much time. So, I must grit my teeth and try not to cover my ears to avoid Dagda's anguished cries of pain as I heal him. Out of the corner of my eye, I see Kallen restraining Kegan. He must believe I am intentionally causing Dagda more harm. He will understand in a moment that I am not.

When it is finally done, I sit back in relief. I seem to be the only one relieved, though. Dagda scrambles away from me, cowering in the corner. It breaks my heart. The fear in his eyes has not eased, it seems to have tripled. What the hell?

"Have you come to heal me so you can think of another form of torture worse than the one imposed by Xenia?" Dagda demands.

I stare at him in shock. When I find my voice, I snark, "Wow, if gratuity was an art form, you would be a mind numbing amateur."

Nonplussed, Dagda stares at me for a long moment. Finally, all he can say is, "What?"

I roll my eyes. "I am not here to hurt you. I am here to rescue you."

This has him shaking his head. "I do not believe you. And even if I did, I will not put young Kegan's life in danger along with mine."

"That is noble and all, but I'm still rescuing you. I'll make sure Kegan isn't hurt."

"No."

Okay, this is getting us nowhere. I reach a hand out toward him and Dagda flinches. Wow, being bound in irons for lord knows how long has definitely made him skittish. Or it could just be me. Regardless, I simply move closer so I can touch him. In a blink, I am back on the other side of the glass with Dagda in tow. He stumbles and Kallen must reach out and grasp him to keep him from falling down.

Kegan shakes his head in wonder. "You are amazing."

I do not like how doe eyed he looks at the moment. Apparently, neither does Kallen. As soon as my husband rights Dagda, he punches his cousin in the arm. Kegan now has pain instead of lust and adoration in his eyes. I give Kallen an appreciative nod. Besides, once Kegan remembers he is married to Alita, he'll feel badly about this moment.

"Put me back!" Dagda hisses.

Scowling, I snark, "Because iron is your color?"

"What?"

I roll my eyes yet again. The Fairy simply does not get my sarcasm. A quick glance around the small room tells me no one else does, either. Oh well.

Tabitha comes to my aid. "We need to get into the archives. We need you to do it. If you want to come back here afterwards, so be it."

I scowl at her. There is no way I am going to let him come back and volunteer to have his lips melted off with iron. I am about to say this when Kallen gently squeezes my shoulder and gives me a pointed look. *Play along* his eyes are telling me. Fine. I'll keep this bit of knowledge to myself. The rest of them will find out soon enough. Instead, I say, "If you all touch my arms, I can simply teleport us to the archives."

Tabitha shakes her head. "No, there may be Xenia's guards there. They routinely attempt to break the spell around the archives."

"Are we just supposed to wait for them to leave if they're around?" I ask.

"What choice do we have?" Kegan responds with a shrug.

Kallen grins at his cousin. "You do not know my wife, do you?" His grin fades as soon as he realizes what he said. Around us, mouths are gaping open. We are not married in this reality. "Soon to be wife," he amends, which still doesn't have their mouths closing.

"How about we move this along," I hurry to say. We have more important things to talk about right now than whether or not Kallen and I are married. Which we definitely are.

"Yes, we should," Tabitha agrees. She is not going to let us off the hook that easily, though. "We will be returning to this topic very soon," she warns and I give her a resigned nod.

Without another word, we enter the hall again. We only come upon a couple of Fairies who work for the palace. Even though they do not scream or run for help when they see that we have freed Dagda, I still feel compelled to take away that option. I send out my magic and put them to sleep. They slip to the floor and are snoozing comfortably by the time we walk by.

"Nice," Kegan whispers.

"Just one of my many talents," I tell him with a wink. This earns me a jealous glower from my husband. I roll my eyes. Like I would flirt with Kegan.

When we finally reach the archives and find the entrance free of Xenia's guards, I turn to Tabitha expectantly. "What now?"

"Now, the two of you lay your hands upon the door," she says.

I nod at the simple brilliance. Since in this reality it was unlikely that Dagda and I would be willing to be in the same place together, let alone on the same side of a battle, who would guess this is what it would take to break the spell. Plus, there is no way Xenia or her guards could ever force me to place my hand upon the door. They simply aren't strong enough. Pure brilliance. I'm going to assume this was my idea.

Dagda takes a step closer but hesitates. He turns to Tabitha. "How do we know for certain which side she is on."

He is accusing me of being a traitor? I open my mouth to rip into him but Kallen speaks first. "She has forgiven you," he says. Now, my mouth drops open even farther.

My eyes shift to Dagda. Is that all it will take for him to believe me?

He doesn't seem to believe it. "Impossible," he says with a furtive glance in my direction. "Not after what I did."

"You mean sending mercenaries to kill me?" I ask. I need to be clear on what I am supposedly forgiving him for. He may have done other things in this reality that may simply be unforgivable. What am I thinking? Nothing that he remembers happening is real and we need to get on with this.

Dagda's eyes are planted firmly on the floor. "Could there be anything worse?"

I snort. "Oh, yeah. I could make a list of things other beings have attempted against me which are much worse than that."

Doubt is written all over Dagda's face, but he pushes forward. "Do you truly forgive me?"

I barely refrain from rolling my eyes. "Yes, now can we get on with it?"

Despite the clear frustration in my voice which could lead one to doubt the sincerity of my words, Dagda nods. He steps to the door and lays his hand upon it. I move forward and do the same. As soon as our hands make contact, a burst of magic shoots forth and surrounds us.

Not all of us. Just me and Dagda. In a flash of light, the two of us are suddenly in the archives. Which startles the hell out of the ancient scribe. He screams and faints dead away. Well, I hope not dead away. I don't like the guy, but I don't want to have inadvertently had something to do with his death twice.

Come to think of it, I guess I never really knew the Fairy. When I had interactions with him before, it wasn't really him. Tana was impersonating him. Great, now I feel even more guilty about the fact we may have just killed him. He could have been a really nice guy for all I know.

Reading my worried expression, Dagda assures me, "He is still breathing." But there's not a lot of conviction in his voice. I think he's just trying to be nice.

15 CHAPTER

Despite his words, Dagda does kneel down and check the scribe for a pulse. We are both relieved when he finds one. Rising, the King glances around. "What are we looking for?"

How much do I tell him? "I need a spell or ritual that will show me a very powerful spell caster and what I can do to stop him or her."

Dagda cocks a brow. "I do not believe one spell or ritual could do both."

"Okay, then one which will expose him so I can stop him however I can."

He studies me a moment. "I assume you believe dark magic is being used, otherwise we would not need to be here."

I nod. "I'm pretty sure. And it is really powerful stuff." I take a deep breath and yet again break the agreement I made with Kallen to keep this between ourselves. The more Dagda knows at this point, the better he is going to be able to help me. "Someone is changing realities. This," I wave my hands in the air, "isn't real. Our lives are much different than this." There, it's out there.

Giving me the same unbelieving, and somewhat pitying, look Tabitha did, Dagda says softly, "I understand that your life has been turned upside down in devastating ways. I am afraid that is your reality now."

I barely restrain a frustrated sigh. "I really do not need a fatherly lecture right now. I need a spell. If you don't believe me, that's fine. In this reality we don't really talk much and you don't know me very well, so why should you believe me? That doesn't change the fact I'm right." As an afterthought, I add, "If it helps motivate you, in the reality I come from you and I have an actual father/daughter relationship. You trying to kill me is a distant memory neither of us dwells on."

Is that a glimmer of hope I see in his eyes? Either that or he is plotting something evil. Or he has gas. I'm going with the hope theory. "Truly?" he asks, his eyes going all soft and puppy doggish.

"Yes, now tell me where to look."

With purposeful strides, Dagda heads toward a section dangerously close to the dark magic section. He looks almost regal as he makes his way down the aisle. He would look even more regal if his clothes weren't hanging in rags from his body. I'd make him new ones but I still try to refrain from that. Changing everyone's outfit in the palace would most certainly alert Xenia of my presence. If any of his unmentionables were hanging out, I'd give it a shot anyway. I shudder at the thought. Thankfully, they're not.

Dagda stops so abruptly, I run into him. He manages to keep from falling by reaching out and grabbing a shelf. He yelps and grabs his hand back when a book seems to bite him. Yes, we really are close to the dark magic section. I'm going to assume we are in the gray magic section right now.

"Are you okay?" I ask, moving to get a closer look at the book that bit him. It has no title but it definitely has teeth in its spine. Creepy.

"I am fine. Do not touch that book."

I roll my eyes. "I am not stupid."

Chagrined, he hurries to say, "I did not mean to imply that you are…"

I wave off his apology. "What book should I be looking at?"

He moves across the aisle and pulls a forest green, leather bound book from the shelf. "I believe you may find what you seek in here." He hands me the book. I take it carefully after assessing it for teeth. I don't find any, thank goodness.

Opening the stiff leather, I leaf through the thick, faded pages hoping a spell will pop out at me. Sometimes, magic books will open to the page you need. Sometimes, they don't. This would be one of those latter times, of course. Frustrated and eternally impatient, I flip back to the front of the book and reluctantly begin to peruse the pages more closely, still hoping something will just pop out at me.

I didn't realize I was pacing until my hair is suddenly holding on for dear life lest it be wrenched permanently from my scalp. Dagda is by my side in an instant, trying to disentangle my hair from the book with teeth. The thing has a death grip, though, and he doesn't have much luck. Meanwhile, I am being pulled closer and closer to it. How? Because the stupid thing didn't just bite my hair, it seems to be swallowing it, too. More and more of my long black hair is disappearing inside the book. I am just a couple of inches from it being able to bite my scalp. How is this not a dark magic book? I suppose there is nothing inherently evil about a book having teeth or thus book eating hair, but still. This is so wrong. Fearing the feel of teeth sinking into my scalp, I do the unthinkable. I lash out with magic. Lots and lots of magic.

Yes, the last time I was here, I used magic. I was a tad bit smarter about it then. I wound commands into my spell which prevented the books and scrolls and whatnot from using my magic to fuel what is written in them. Yeah, I didn't do that this time. Kallen's fear of my destroying the archives pops back into my head. Damn, I hate it when I prove him right.

Shrieks and howls erupt in the musty air. Dust flies as books flop from the shelves in their eagerness to open and let loose their contents. The sound of tearing and crackling paper is all around us. Smoke begins to rise from several aisles as some of the tomes set on fire. I assume from conflicting spells struggling for control of the magic that is being pulled through me. I am losing control of it. I drop to my knees as I struggle to stop the flow of magic being ripped through me, but I can't tamp it back down. There's simply too much of it.

Dagda drops to his own knees before me. He attempts to grab my shoulders but I scoot away, not letting him make contact. Too dangerous at the moment. "Xandra!" he shouts.

"I'm not deaf," I inform him over the shrieking around us. Oh, maybe he did need to yell.

"Fight it!" he tells me.

Does he realize how much that makes me want to feed him to one of the darker books? "I am!" I growl back.

His eyes flit to the floor and then back to me. A grin forms on his face and I'm convinced for a moment that he has gone completely bonkers. "Then channel it," he says.

I have no idea what he's talking about until my eyes follow his to the floor. The book I was holding a moment ago is lying there. Open to a particular page. I guess it just took another book eating my hair to activate whatever it is that makes a magic book open to the right page. Or it was just dumb luck. I'm going with the hair eating theory.

As soon as Dagda is convinced I understand, he backs off. Rising to his feet, he moves back several feet until his back is almost touching the row of books behind him. He's smart enough not to get too close to the book shelf. He likes his scalp and who knows how many more books with teeth there are here.

Grabbing the book, I don't bother to stand. The book with teeth that let go of my hair when I flung magic at it snaps at me and I kick it away. Sitting with my legs crisscross, I put the spell book in my lap and read aloud the words on the page. *"Wickedness lurks in the shadows, biding its time in the hedgerow. Casting forth its ugly magic, waiting for consequences tragic. Fighting this darkness will take heart, winning may wrench this soul apart. I will fight black to black, harnessing evil in my counterattack. Use the darkness to bring to light, the mastermind of my plight. Expose and twist with iron fist. Bring me now this black hearted fool whether he be Angel or ancient Ghoul. Entangle him in this mire of evil and sin, trap him now here within. Trap him in evil's embrace, no longer allowed to torture and abase."*

Okay, I am still going to blow up the archives. The shrieking reaches a crescendo. A tornado like wind erupts through the aisles. I cover my head to avoid having falling books crush my skull. Dagda reaches a hand out to pull me out of harm's way but I wave him off. "Don't touch me!" I shout. The hurt in his eyes cuts deep. He doesn't realize if he touches me, the magic being wrenched through me will take a detour through him. "The magic will use you!" I try to explain. He still doesn't get it, but he now has an idea that maybe it wasn't personal. He nods and backs off. Meanwhile, a book clunks onto my skull because I am too busy explaining myself than making sure I don't get knocked unconscious. I scowl at Dagda even though it wasn't really his fault.

My eyes are ripped from my biological father by what is happening in the main aisle of the archives. Scrambling to my feet, I rush to get a better view with Dagda on my heels. A black cloud is forming. Magic from all corners of the archives are coalescing, converging, creating a powerful darkness that roils with energy. And any second now, it's going to explode and destroy us all, I just know it.

Then again, I do have a tendency to be wrong sometimes. The energy, the dark magic, doesn't explode. It actually seems to be shrinking. Dagda and I watch in fascination as this great cloud of dark energy grows ever smaller. The magic being pulled through me is still so powerful I am having trouble remaining on my feet, but I am in too much awe to fall down.

After several long minutes, a form starts to take shape within the swirling blackness. A misshapen being. Its shrieks and howls replace that of the books and scrolls. It overpowers them, quiets them as if they know they are inadequate compared to this…this thing before me. As it comes into focus, its own howling begins to quiet. Its eyes find me and it roars in a voice so sharp and loud, I feel my eardrums burst and my nose begins to bleed.

I force myself not to wipe at the blood dripping toward my lips. I don't cover my ears. Because I know in my heart that if I show any sign of weakness, I'm dead.

16 Chapter

The creature has come into sharp focus now. It's tall, lanky form is hunched over, a hump on its back making it impossible to stand straight. It takes me a moment to determine that its skin is actually black, it's not a trick of the dark smoke and energy swirling around it. Its eyes are glowing silver and red alternately, pulsing and changing colors as its fury grows. Its teeth are fangs with long, sharp incisors hanging out of its mouth. Its head is bald, the skin on it wrinkled and cracked. It looks as if it has spent years in a fire pit, slow roasting like a pig at a luau. Just not in such a cheery situation. I suspect this creature comes straight from the bowels of hell.

"What are you?" I ask barely above a whisper. I really don't expect it to answer me. How could such a thing be capable of speech?

It does answer me. It's voice crawls along my skin. "I am one of many," it hisses.

That doesn't bode well for me, I'm sure. "Then why did the spell bring only you?" I ask. Hmm. Asking my enemy to explain how a spell I cast works. That doesn't make me look silly at all. Besides that, the answer comes to me all on its own. "Because you were the one casting the reality spell." Look at me, I'm a genius. If only I could have figured that out before I let slip that I don't always understand my magic. Never a good thing to admit to one's enemy.

The creature doesn't say anything more. I'll take his silence as confirmation. Looking more closely at it, I decide I can't really tell if it's male or female. There's still too much smoke and magic surrounding it. Regardless of its gender, it is one ugly beast. It is fighting against the magic holding it, focusing all of its attention on this. In fact, it seems to have forgotten Dagda and me altogether.

As if his name crossing my mind suddenly sparked his ability to speak, Dagda whispers, "I did not truly believe they exist."

I sigh in frustration. "Do you know how many times I've heard you say that?"

Surprised, he turns to me. "There are other beings of legend you have discovered?"

I am not getting into that discussion at the moment. I shouldn't have even brought it up because now my biological father's curiosity is going to be eating at him. It better not affect his ability to fight if need be. "Let's just concentrate on this one. What is it?"

Dagda's eyes move back to the dark being. "I believe it is a Demon." He shakes his head in disbelief. "I know not what else it could be."

"A Demon?" I groan. "Really?" I remember a conversation a long time ago about Demons. I could have sworn Kallen told me they don't exist. Or, did he just imply that? Doesn't matter now, I suppose, because here one is.

"As I have never seen one before, I cannot be certain. It does fit the general description, though."

"We'll go with Demon then. How do I get rid of it?"

This gets the creature's attention. "You think to vanquish me, precious Witch Fairy of the Angels?"

Putting my hands on my hips, I nod. "That was the general idea."

A snarl curls its almost nonexistent lip over its fangs. "I am not a lower being such as yourself. My magic holds upon my death."

Meaning I'd be trapped in this reality if I do actually vanquish him. Casting a sidelong glance at Dagda, I say out of the corner of my mouth, "I assume Demons lie."

He nods. "I would assume so."

Great. Returning my attention to the Demon, I say, "I don't believe you."

"Then vanquish me now."

I would. I really would. If only I knew how. Which I don't. I bet there's a book in here somewhere which would tell me how, but I doubt the Demon is going to wait patiently for me to find it. Thinking back to Demon lore in my realm, I try another tack. "Are you bound by the deals you make?"

"Xandra," Dagda says in his best 'don't make stupid deals with Demons' voice. That's a new one. He's pretty good at rolling with the flow with these things in any reality, I guess.

Ignoring Dagda, I ask again, "Are you bound by the deals you make?" The Demon still does not answer me. I suspect this is because the thing does not want to admit to what I am beginning to believe in my heart. If it makes a deal with me, it cannot for whatever reason, go back on its word. "I thought as much," I say smugly. Too smugly, I am sure. It'll come back and bite me in the ass, I know it will. And it'll leave teeth marks. Long, deep teeth marks probably shaped like Demon fangs. Okay, now I am totally grossed out by the idea of a Demon biting me in the butt. But, I don't know what else to do at the moment. What can I do besides make a deal with him? When I thought about casting the spell, I certainly didn't expect a Demon to show up, so obviously I didn't research what to do with it when it did. Basically, I'm stuck in a stalemate and I'm screwed. Unless I make a deal.

"You cannot hold me with this trifling magic indefinitely," the Demon hisses.

I study him for a long time before speaking. He has slowed in his fight against the magic. Not because he knows he is close to winning, but because he is tired. And because he knows his attempts are futile. I most certainly can hold him indefinitely with this magic. Except, that would require me spending my life here in the archives doing just that. Which isn't going to work for me.

"You will cease altering realities and return everything to what it was before you cast your spell. You will leave me and everyone I know and care about alone. You will leave this place and never come back. You will never again use magic in this realm or any other realm in this universe. You will forget you even know who I am. If you agree to this, I will let you go."

"Xandra, you cannot," Dagda hisses.

I turn to him and throw up my hands. "Then what do you suggest? I hold him here for eternity?"

Pressing his lips in a thin line, Dagda remains silent. I've actually shut him up. That never happens. He always has an opinion to add. Not this time. Must be the time he spent in iron in this reality wore him down.

"I accept your terms."

Oops, I forgot about the Demon. Hmm. He acquiesced rather quickly. And with no counter demands. That cannot be a good thing. On the other hand, I do not feel even a tingle on my skin indicating the thing is lying.

"The deal has been made. You must release me," the Demon insists. What his lips are doing now is probably supposed to be a smug smile, but it's too horrific to even closely resemble one. "Unless you do not keep your word, daughter of the Angels."

Funny, a Demon calling my word into question doesn't really bother me. But, I suspect that my Angel blood would not be happy if I went back on my word. Which is why he called me daughter of the Angels. Not to mention that pesky fact that I need to release him eventually anyway. Eying him, I can't help but ask, "What is the catch? What did I miss when making my deal?"

The creepy smile gets even wider proving beyond doubt that I made a terrible mistake in judgement here. I was only able to see its awful yellow front teeth before. Now I can see its even awful more awful brown back teeth as it grins at me. "I am not the only one," he cackles.

Damn. I forgot about that. "I suppose your friends will be coming for me, then."

"Not just you."

I hope that wasn't supposed to make me feel better. "Why? What did I do to you?"

"You are distorting the balance."

"What does that mean?"

"You know what it means," the Demon hisses. "There must be balance of dark and light."

My mouth drops open. "You mean I am bringing too much good into the universe? But, that's my job!"

"And this is mine," he hisses. "Now, release me."

"So that your buddies can keep coming after me?"

"That is no longer my concern. I have made my deal with you and shall abide by it. What befalls you after this is of your own doing."

"Comforting," I mutter. Straightening my shoulders, I bolster my courage to follow through with this stupid deal I made. "When I release you, what happens?"

"Your reality is restored."

"Intact?" I ask. "Everything will be exactly the same?"

"Yes," the Demon hisses. "Everything outside of this room will be the same."

My eyes flit to Dagda. He shrugs his shoulders as if to say, I have nothing to add. Helpful. I look back at the Demon. "Fine. Go."

I suck in a breath as the magic is yanked back through me. It feels like sludge as the bits of dark magic attached to it filter through me on their way back to their books and scrolls. All I can think as this happens is, at least I didn't blow up the archives. I came pretty close to destroying it, but I didn't blow it up. I am still reeling in this wonderful fact when the Demon pops out of existence.

Dagda reaches out a steadying hand and shakes his head. "I will never doubt anything you say ever again." Well. That's nice.

"That probably won't last," I mutter.

Suddenly ashen, Dagda wipes a hand over his face and groans loudly, "Tana is going to kill me. Perhaps we can bring the Demon back?"

I almost laugh because he just might be serious. I suspect he now remembers the last few days and all that he did during them. Interesting. With the magic gone, they must all remember their actions now. I wonder how Mom's taking it. Glad I'm not with her at the moment. She's probably as horrified as I was when I saw her and Dagda kissing. Okay, I snicker a little bit. I blame it on the stress of the last few days. Really.

17 CHAPTER

The door to the archives slams open and Kallen, Kegan and Tabitha charge through them. I gape at the trio. Their clothes are torn, there's blood on Tabitha's arm and several bruises on Kegan. Kallen doesn't look injured, but he does look exhausted.

"What happened?" I ask.

"Xenia's guards," Kallen responds. He glances around the archives. "What happened in here? I thought perhaps there was another tornado. I see I may not have been far off."

The magic may have returned to wherever it comes from, but the archives are still a disaster. "Demon," I tell him, hoping that will distract him from the 'I told you so' which is probably dancing on his lips at the moment.

It does. His gorgeous green eyes grow large with disbelief. "Demon?" His eyes go to the King for confirmation. I'd be insulted but I did just throw the idea of Demons at him. Who wouldn't have doubts?

"I would not believe it myself if I had not seen it with my own eyes," Dagda says behind me. "But it was, in fact, a Demon."

"Impossible," Tabitha claims with a wave of her arm. "They were all destroyed ages before the first Fairy was born."

"Apparently, someone missed a few," I grumble.

"A few? There was more than one?" Kallen asks.

I shake my head. "No, just the one, but he said there are more."

"Hey, if you guys have things covered here, I'd really like to find Alita and Keelan," Kegan says, anxiety crawling all over his handsome features.

Guilt washes over me. Of course he wants to find his wife and child now that he remembers they exist. "Go," I tell him. "We got this." He doesn't wait for anyone else to respond. Kegan tears out of the archives in search of his family.

Now that I think about it, Alita wasn't present in any of the realities. I wonder why. In a massive 'duh' moment, it comes to me. She is a walking dark magic detector. She would have given it all away. Fear washes over me. Did the Demon harm her to keep her from alerting us? I meet Kallen's eyes and know that the same thought is going through his mind.

We are not alone in this. "Follow him," Tabitha orders. "Make sure she is okay."

I reach out and grab Kallen's hand. "My way is quicker." As soon as I make contact with his skin, we are standing in front of the ocean side cottage where Alita's parents live.

Her father is pacing outside. He looks up when he senses us and relief washes over him. "Is it over?" he asks.

"Yes," I assure him, though I'm not certain what 'over' means to him. "Is she okay?" He knows I mean Alita, not his wife even though I hope she is fine, as well.

"She has been near death's door for three days. She would not eat or drink while she was conscious she was so ill. The babe had to be bottle fed."

A wave of guilt washes over me. That first day this all began, when I took a walk on the beach, I chose to avoid this small cottage. I thought it would be upsetting to Alita for me to come to her with tales of her and Kegan being together with a child. If I hadn't turned and walked the other way, I would have found her in this state. I would have known then that something involving dark magic was occurring. I would have found Keelan alive and well and proof that I wasn't crazy. Maybe I could have saved them both some suffering. On the other hand, I still would not have known what was causing this to happen. Not until I found that book in the archives. I'm also sure there would have been obstacles put in place to postpone me finding Alita as long as possible.

"How is she now?" Kallen asks.

A smile breaks through the worry on Alita's father's face. "She is awake and her headache is gone. A bit of color is returning to her face." Storm clouds form in his eyes. "She has been asking for Kegan, but he has not been about."

I peek at Kallen. Did just our realities change, those of us who live at Isla's and the palace? Or did this cottage get spared only because of Alita? Kallen gives me a slight shrug in reply. He doesn't know any better than I do.

Kallen is the one to respond to the accusation in the older Fairy's voice. "Kegan has been helping us fight a new enemy these past days. I am afraid he was not able to send word."

"He's on his way now, though," I assure Alita's father. I suppose I should have found him and teleported him, too. That would have been the nice thing to do. From Kallen's chagrined expression, he has realized this belatedly, as well. Oops. We were just in such a hurry to make sure Alita and Keelan were alive and well.

It's not too late. With a significant glance at Kallen to let him know what I am going to do, I teleport again. This time, I am on the path we take when walking from Isla's to the palace. I don't know how far along Kegan will be, so I hope I didn't miss him. He was moving pretty fast when he ran out of the palace. I am relieved when I see him tearing through the forest about fifty yards away. He sees me and stops. I teleport closer and he has to reach out and keep me from falling when I land on an exposed tree root. As soon as I have my balance, I teleport us back to the beach cottage. Kegan is inside in a heartbeat, not even a glance spared for Alita's father. The older Fairy isn't insulted. He smiles after his son-in-law and walks back into the house himself.

Kallen and I follow them inside. We make our way to Alita's old bedroom and knock on the open doorframe. Kegan has his wife in a tight embrace. Alita peeks over

Kegan's shoulder and waves us in. She is pale, but she is sitting up. Whether on her own or because Kegan is holding her upright, I'm not certain, but I suspect much of her weakness has passed since the Demon's demise. Next to the bed, a baby begins to cry. Kegan gently removes his arms from Alita and moves to him, scooping his son into his arms and holding him close. Not too close. He's careful not to smother him, babies being fragile and all that. Alita is staring at both of them with pure, unadulterated love radiating from her eyes.

Reluctant to interrupt this tender scene, Kallen and I do need to go. We have a lot of family and friends to round up. But, I don't want to leave until I am certain Alita and the baby are fine. "Do you need me to heal you?" I ask her.

Alita shakes her head. "No, I feel much better." Her eyes move back to Kegan. "I assume you can tell me what has been going on?" she asks her husband.

Kegan is too busy checking Keelan over to respond. Not finding any obvious injuries, he finally asks Alita, "Does he require healing?"

Shaking her head again, she reassures him softly, "He is fine, as well. Mama and Papa have made certain of it."

Relief washes over Kegan. Finally, he answers Alita's question, "I am not certain I understand all of it, but I will certainly try to explain."

I open my mouth to offer to move them back home but close it again. They may be safer here. Alita was out of the changing reality loop, as were her parents. I glance at Kallen and he nods in agreement. I love that he so often knows what I'm thinking.

"We will leave the two of you then. We need to find the others who have been missing these past few days," Kallen says. He takes my hand, but before I teleport us away, he adds, "Stay here, Cousin. This may be the safest place for you and your family right now."

Wrapping an arm around Alita's shoulders, Kegan nods. "Let me know if you need help."

"We will," Kallen lies. There is no way in hell we are going to tear apart this family again.

Kegan is not stupid. He knows his cousin too well. "I have more to fight for than I ever have before," he insists. "Do not leave me from the battle because you fear separating us."

Alita's eyes are wide with fear, but she concurs. "If Kegan is needed, he needs to fight."

"We are not fighting Centaurs or Sasquatch, we are fighting Demons," I tell her.

I feel guilty when she blanches. "Demons?" she echoes.

I nod. "And considering they are the epitome of evil, we think Kegan's place is right here protecting you and the baby." When she opens her mouth to object, I add, "I've been in the presence of one. You've only been on the periphery of its magic. I don't think you would survive being up and close and personal." Blunt, but true. "Right now, I believe you need a body guard more so than we need Kegan's help on our end. If that changes, we will let you know."

Kegan is torn. He wants to argue, but his eyes keep darting between Alita and the baby. Kallen reaches out and squeezes his cousin's shoulder. "We will call upon you if we truly need your help." This time, it's not a lie. Understanding this, Kegan nods. He will not argue any more about it.

Now that we are all in agreement, it's time to go home, round everyone else up, and figure out what the hell we are going to do about the Demons who are after us.

18 Chapter

Not sure what to expect, I teleport us to the beach instead of inside the house. I doubt there are traps waiting for us, but I did make a deal with a Demon without knowing all the rules. I basically went on ideas I've gleaned from TV shows, books and movies. That being said, he may not be quite as trustworthy as I hope he is.

Kallen is just as leery as I am and he doesn't even know all the details of what happened yet. I haven't had a chance to explain the stupid deal I made. "Do you believe it safe to enter?" he asks. "Will the Demon return?"

Before I have a chance to respond, the terrace door is traversed by several beings. Fortunately, all of them are friendly. Mom and Dad hurry through first, followed by

Isla and Garren. I glance over their shoulders waiting for Adriel and Raziel. They do not appear. Strange.

"Xandra!" Mom throws her arms around me and sobs. Not in relief. She is just sobbing. Um, this is weird. Mom is never this emotional. Dad comes close to us, but he doesn't make it a group hug. There is something lurking in his eyes, something which puts a lump in my throat and what feels like a pile of dead flies in my belly. It's pain in his eyes. The pain of betrayal. Oh god, he knows. He knows what happened between Dagda and Mom. No wonder Mom is crying. I bet a big part of it is embarrassment, but the rest I am certain is because she would never intentionally hurt Dad.

"Dad…" I begin, but he shakes his head. Kallen puts a hand on my shoulder, shaking his head slightly, too. "Not now," he says softly. It didn't take him any longer than it took me to realize what the problem is.

"Come inside," Isla insists, scanning the horizon. "I believe explanations are in order, but I do not believe it wise to remain in the open like this."

Peeling Mom from my arms takes a minute. It also takes Kallen's help. He reaches out and gently pulls her limbs back like layers of an onion. One at a time. "We need to focus on a plan," he says to her softly. "The battle is not yet won." Mom nods and sniffles, wiping the tears from her eyes.

Dad clearly wants to reach out to her, but he's not ready for that yet. I want to ask him how he knows. Did Mom immediately come out of her haze of false memories and confess what happened? If so, I appreciate her honesty, but maybe she should have waited for explanations before admitting her guilt. That probably would have helped ease Dad's pain. Or, maybe we could have just skipped over that little unpleasantness. After all, it wasn't her fault. She probably couldn't have lived with the guilt, though. I know I wouldn't have been able to live with it.

"Where is Zac?" I ask my parents. Their pain aside, I need to know my brother is safe.

"He is in his room. I insisted he stay there until we have time to sort things out," Dad says. With a covert glance at Mom, he adds, "He is very confused right now. I thought it best he not be here." I'm not certain I agree. And, I hate the fact that he is alone. But, maybe Dad has a point. Zac is close by so we can hear him if he's in trouble, and being around our parents right now may not be the best thing for him.

The six of us make our way into the house. We head straight for the kitchen. Not because we're hungry. I, for one, would probably gag on food at the moment the way my stomach is churning bile. But, because the kitchen is where we always meet when we are dealing with a crisis. Or pretty much anything else. Taking seats at the island counter, we sit in a stunned silence for a moment. Isla and Garren are giving Dad pitying glances, so apparently they know, as well. Did Mom share with them, too? Did she make a general announcement or something? That seems unnaturally cruel of her. What the hell is going on?

Being me, of course I ask. "Mom, why didn't you wait to tell Dad what happened with you and Dagda?" There is more accusation in my voice than I meant for there to be. I can't help it, though. We may have been able to avoid the pain Dad, who flinches at the mention of the Fairy King's name, is now feeling. It was selfish of her to try to wash away her guilt by jumping into premature confessions and I'm starting to feel a lot less sorry for her and a lot more annoyed.

"She did not tell me," Dad says quietly. "I saw." Well, that shuts up my inner monologue regarding my mother and how she should have done things differently.

"You saw?" Kallen echoes. "What do you mean?"

"I assume you are aware of the shifting in realities?" Isla asks.

I try not to roll my eyes. "Since I am the only one who was aware during all of them, yes." Hmm, maybe I shouldn't be so snarky. She might not know that.

Or, maybe she does. Slightly chagrined, Isla says, "Of course."

"You observed?" Kallen echoes. He is starting to sound like a parrot.

"Good god, let us put it out there already," Garren gripes. Looking at Kallen and me, he explains, "When one of us was not forced to participate in a reality, we were forced to watch. We retained our memories from our reality to make any betrayals," his eyes shift to Dad, "all the more painful." A shudder runs down his spine. That is downright cruel of the Demons. Then again, they are Demons. What else would they do, have picnics in the park all day and then rock everyone to sleep at night singing loving lullabies? "Who knows what was in store for the rest of us if it continued," Garren adds. He reaches over and takes Isla's hand in his and gives it a squeeze. I suspect images of Isla's first husband are flashing through his mind and what it would have been like to watch her with him.

Kallen is as aghast as I am. "They made you watch? How?"

"It was like watching television," Dad explains. Kallen and I get it. Garren is a bit confused. Fairies have a vague idea of such things in the Cowan realm, but only those I've brought there recently really understand modern technology.

"And you were all together in a room watching when it wasn't your turn to be a part of the show?" How creepy is that?

Lips forming a grim line, Dad nods. "Yes."

"Good to know that no matter how many realities you live through, you are still Queen of the Obvious," a snarky voice says from my ankle.

Despite his annoying comment, I want to hug him. "Taz! Where have you been?"

"We were checking the perimeter," another voice low to the floor says.

I beam at my other Familiar. "Felix."

Felix's eyes are trained on the floor. "My apologies."

It takes me a moment to realize why he is apologizing. "For that other reality?" I ask.

"Queen of the..." I don't let Taz finish before kicking out at him.

"Hush," I tell him. To Felix, I say, "No apologies. That was a different reality and your memories were all screwed up. It's okay. You didn't have all the memories we've made since you left that other universe." My eyes climb from Felix to my Dad. He needs to hear the same thing. Well, not the alternate universe part, but pretty much the same thing. He looks so sad my heart is breaking for him. "Dad, you must know that these realities seemed real to everyone in them. Memories were implanted or changed and no one had any control over it. It was like everyone had lived those lives all along. Even you forgot that you delivered Keelan just the day before," I point out.

Dad's eyes narrow. "You were never under the Demon's spell. Perhaps the rest of us are simply weaker of mind than you are." God, I hope not. I really rely on the strength of mind of those around me. It would suck to find out it's all been a sham. Good thing I'm confident he's wrong.

Kallen's brow scrunches into a vee. "You know about the Demons?" Oh, yeah. We haven't had a chance to explain our side of things yet. How does Dad know a Demon did all this?

"The Demon showed himself to us," Isla explains. "He did not ever make himself corporeal so we could fight him, but he made his presence known. He explained what he was doing."

"Bloody bastard wanted to take credit for the torture he was meting out," Garren snarls.

"Was he planning to let it go on forever?" I ask.

Isla nods. "I believe that was the original intent." A tiny smile touches her lips. "I believe he underestimated your stubbornness and determination, though. He did not believe you would not only be able to convince others of what was happening, but also find a way to stop it."

"He was hopping mad when you destroyed his last reality," Taz chuckles. "You were so good, I almost like you now."

I glower at him. "You love me."

Taz sniffs. "Don't get carried away." I'll take that as a confirmation.

"He definitely underestimated the power you wield," Dad says, his lips forming a smile that doesn't quite reach his eyes. "A mistake he won't make again."

I shrug. "Doesn't matter for him. He agreed to leave us alone." Before anyone gets too excited, I add, "Too bad he says he has lots of friends."

Isla scowls. "A Demon army has been reborn?"

I shrug again. "I don't know if it's an army, but he said there are more." Getting back to what they've shared, I do a quick recap. "So, let me get this straight. A Demon kept all of you in what was essentially a Green Room until you were needed to play a part in his sick, and meant to be eternal, game of changing realities? All because the Angels want me to bring more goodness to the universe than evil?"

Nonplussed, Garren asks, "Green Room?"

Isla frowns and asks at the same time, "What is this about the Angels?"

I finally take the opportunity to fill them in on my trip to the archives and the conversation I had with the Demon. They knew about the archive thing, but apparently, once I pulled the Demon to me, they could no longer see what was going on. I suppose the Demon didn't want them to see his weakness.

"You know, you probably should have led with that information," Taz says from where he is trying to nudge the pantry door open.

"I didn't have a chance," I inform him.

He peeks at my Mom over his shoulder then puts his nose back to the task of opening the door. "Yeah, I guess some drama got in your way. Stupid mortals and their petty feelings."

"You only say that because you don't have a girlfriend," I tease.

"Could we please get back to this discussion instead of that your Familiar's love life?" Isla drawls. Wow, a few days as a Demon hostage and she gets snippy.

Before I can make a snippy comment of my own, the back door slams open. Tana in all her furious glory stalks in. Reflexively, I pull magic. When her stormy green eyes fly to my mother, I pull more magic. When she turns and flings herself into my Dad's arms and begins to cry, I am too stunned to hold onto my magic and it all slips away. What the hell? Even Taz's mouth drops open. Felix, however, is still on guard in case he needs to bite someone. Namely, Tana.

Dad, clearly uncomfortable, still does his best to comfort her. "It wasn't real," he reassures her, patting her back awkwardly. If only he felt that way himself, then he would sound like he meant it.

"But, even your daughter realized that none of our personalities could be altered to the point that we would do things or be with others we despised. Kallen would never have been with Xenia," Tana whines into his chest.

She is making a huge mess of Dad's t-shirt and he is trying hard not to notice. He does grimace toward the growing wet spot on the front of his shirt once or twice, though.

When I feel Kallen pull magic again, I groan out loud. Tana may not be here to kill my mother, but when Dagda finds his wife in my Dad's arms, he might not be as willing to set aside his homicidal tendencies. For the second time in two minutes, I pull magic and prepare for a fight. I am again shocked into dropping my magic when I witness a reaction that does not at all fall into character with someone I know and love. All Dagda does is stand in the doorway looking defeated. Wow, when did my family stop being sociopaths? Huh, maybe we needed a visit from Demons years ago if this is the outcome. Nah, not really. I'll take sociopathic relatives over Demons any day.

"Tana?" Dagda says tentatively.

"Go away!" she snarls and her eyes spark with intended violence. I may have spoken too soon about her putting her homicidal tendencies away. Best to keep magic at the ready.

While their drama is playing out, another thought hits me. I turn to Kallen. "Why don't you remember being in this room watching everyone?"

"I was never there," he says simply. "I was with you in every reality."

Oh, yeah. He was. "That's strange. I wonder why the Demon didn't try to separate us."

Kallen wraps an arm around my waste and pulls me close. "Because he could not." He gives me a light kiss. Unfortunately, his words just serve to make Tana, and Mom again, cry harder.

"For the love of Bacon!" Taz cries over their combined noise. "Can't you shut them up? My eardrums are bleeding!"

I could give it a shot. It is pretty annoying. Biting my lip, I decide on the best course of action. Do I simply take their voices away? That seems really insensitive. Not to mention, likely to piss both of them off.

To my surprise, it is Kallen who shocks them both out of tears. "Enough already!" His voice booms around the kitchen, echoing off the walls and making the pots and pans hanging from a rack swing in the sonic breeze. "This is exactly what the Demon was trying to do! Yes, Dagda and Julienne were once attracted to each other. Yes, if things had been different, maybe they would have been together. But things were not different. Dagda wanted to be back here with Tana and Julienne found love with Jim. Get the hell over it already so we can move on!"

I stare at him in awe. He's honestly annoyed by how they're behaving. But did my husband just say get the hell over it already? Because I know for a fact that he would not be able to get the hell over it if he found me with someone else. Not right away, anyway. Then again, I've never been with anyone but him so there were no old boyfriends…or lovers as the case may be for Mom and Dagda. And the only other Fairy with any claims on Kallen, real or not, was Xenia. So, the Demon didn't really have this option when it came to us, even though he did give it a valiant effort by bringing in Xenia. But, if we did have pasts with other people and were thrown into them under the Demon's spell, Kallen is right. We would have to suck it up and get the hell over it right away so we could come up with a solution.

"Kallen is correct," Isla concurs with my mental ramblings. "I am certain, given enough time, the Demon would have found a way to drive wedges between all of us. If you four let the Demons be so successful this early in the game, then what hope do we have? Is your love for each other not strong enough to weather something so absurd as the illogical possibility that life could have turned out differently for the four of you?"

Love advice from Isla seems kind of weird. After all, look at how long it took her to admit she loved Garren. Then, look at the fact that she loves Garren. Not exactly the cream of the crop. But, I am not going to point out either of these things because she seems to have helped knock some sense into the four of them. Tears are dried, hugs between spouses are given. Dirty looks and sharp insults are temporarily packed away for the possibility of further use later.

"I'm going to vomit," Taz chokes, trying not to inhale the love in the air.

"Shut up," I admonish.

"No, seriously, he is going to vomit," Felix informs me, rushing to his friend's side.

He's right. Taz wasn't just being snarky like I thought. He starts making these sounds like he's about to hack up a hairball. I am off my stool and by his side in an instant. "Did you eat something?" I demand, wondering if he's choking on a scrap of food and I need to figure out how to give the Heimlich to a Tasmanian devil.

"No," Taz rasps.

His little chest is racked with coughs. After a particularly long coughing spell, he finally vomits. What comes up is a combination of bile and blood. Nasty. Pulling him into my lap, I run a soothing hand through his fur as I pull magic. I don't know what's wrong, but I suspect whatever is happening to him is Demon related. The others in the kitchen have gathered around.

"What is wrong?" Kallen asks, kneeling next to me but keeping a safe distance from me and my magic. And the bloody vomit on the floor.

"I don't know." Sending my magic out to my Familiar, I assess him for injury. My magic can't sense anything physical that is causing his illness. It can, however, sense dark magic trying to weave its slimy tentacles around him. My eyes fly around the room in search of the Demon attacking Taz. I don't see anyone. Not a surprise. I didn't see the other Demon for days while it was wreaking havoc on my life. Not until I called it forth. Glancing around at the others, I warn, "There's a Demon close by."

All eyes suddenly shift from me to everywhere else. They are scanning the area, searching for the invisible Demon. Someone goes outside to look around but I don't pay attention as to who. I keep my attention focused on Taz. I need to disentangle him from this dark magic which is trying to kill him. It dawns on me that we should have spent less time talking about my parents' sex lives and more time figuring out how Demon magic works. Because I don't have the first clue. Which could mean the difference between keeping Taz alive and watching him die.

19 CHAPTER

Taz is not going to die. My head whips toward Felix. "Do you know anything about Demons?" He often knows things about dark magic that none of the rest of us do. It's sometimes handy that my doppelganger in his universe was evil. Well, it's handy for me, of course, not for him. It sucked for him.

"Demons were a thing of the past in our universe, as well," Felix informs me, dashing my hope. My optimism returns when his little eyes light up. "You used the dark magic of the archives to capture the Demon."

I'm not following. "Yes, I did," I say slowly, hoping to catch up. I don't. I still don't know what he's implying. Losing patience when he doesn't say anything else, I growl down at him, "Just spell it out, Felix. Don't make me guess."

"We are made from dark magic."

By spell it out, I guess what I really meant was draw me a picture of exactly what he wants me to do. I open my mouth to tell him this when I realize I may not be as slow as I think I am. "You want me to use the dark magic within Taz to fight the dark magic of the Demon attacking him?"

If Tasmanian devils could grin maniacally, Felix would be doing so right now. "Exactly," he says with an excited bob of his head. Felix never gives excited bobs of his head. He must really believe this will work.

Latching onto his enthusiasm, I give it a shot. The others in the room have taken up defensive stances around us, magic pulled and ready for a fight. "You guys should give me some space," I warn, my attention still on Taz.

Kallen sends me a worried look. "What are you about to do?" He must not have been following my conversation with Felix. He is on hyper alert for a Demon presence, after all. Or, he was following my conversation with Felix and that's why he's worried. Yeah, it's probably the latter.

"Something that is probably dangerous and stupid," I reply honestly. To my surprise, Kallen doesn't argue. He just gives me a nod and moves back. He knows how important Taz is to me, even if I do spend most of my time complaining about him.

Taking a deep breath, I let the words to a spell form in my mind. *"Darkness buried deep inside, swirl up now like an ocean's tide. Fight a battle with magic akin, be the yang to its yin. External forces seek to destroy, this life given by darkness' octroy. Our magic entwined we oust this foe, possession of you it will never know."*

I squeeze my eyes closed against the tearing and pulling of magic as it is sucked through me and combines with my Familiar's. Taz's body bucks and twists. He howls and coughs and spits out more blood. But under it all, I feel him fighting. Not just him. I feel the magic that holds him together. The magic that binds us. I feel it curling and twisting, melding with mine. But, the Demon magic is strong. It's hold on Taz considerable. And I'm not certain we can break through it.

There is a new pressure on my leg. A tiny paw pressing against me. I glance down as Felix flings his other front paw onto Taz. As soon as contact with both of us is made, his grunts of pain join ours. But, when his magic mingles with ours, bolstering it, making it stronger, I know we've won. The hold the Demons have on Taz begins to slip. Like prying fingers from a ledge, the three of us fight to send the Demon magic spiraling back down to the hell from which it was spawned. When the last of it is finally ripped away, the three of us slump to the floor in a furry heap. Not that I've suddenly grown fur, I'm just covered in Tasmanian devil at the moment.

"Xandra!" Kallen is next to me again, his hands on my cheeks. "Are you okay? Are you conscious?"

Those questions probably should have been asked in the reverse order, but he's so worried at the moment I'm not going to point that out. "I'm fine," I mumble through Felix's fur.

Reaching out, Kallen gently lifts Felix away from my face so I can speak. "Better?" he asks.

I nod. "Thanks. How are they?"

Now that he knows I'm fine, Kallen looks my Familiars over. "Out cold, but breathing."

Extending a hand, I say, "Help me up, please." Kallen helps me into a sitting position. He keeps an arm around me to prevent me from falling back down. "That is some wicked stuff," I mutter.

Kallen chuckles softly. "No pun intended?"

"Oh no, definitely pun intended." I put a hand to my stomach. "I'm kind of nauseous myself now."

Quirking a brow, Kallen asks, "Are you going to vomit?"

I consider his question a second before shaking my head. "No." There is a considerable amount of relief in my charming husband's eyes at the moment. So much so, I'm tempted to tell him I changed my mind to tease him. That would be cruel after just scaring the hell out of him for the umpteenth time, though. Okay, we are probably way past even that nonsensical number.

Peering down at me with an expression as worried as Kallen's, Dagda asks, "Are they gone?"

"As far as I can tell," I assure him. He doesn't appear assured. In fact, he narrows his eyes at me, ready to demand that I be more reassuring.

"If she can no longer sense the Demon magic, they must be gone," Kallen insists. Aw, he's so cute when he's defending me. I reach a hand up and lay it against his cheek and smile.

"I appreciate your loyalty, but I do not necessarily believe one absolutely follows the other," Dagda retorts. He is not cute when he is doubting me.

Rising slowly to my feet, I glower at my father. "Well, that's the best I can tell you. If you want a better answer, scan for the magic yourself."

Is that a blush blooming on the Fairy King's face? Why, I do believe it is. I understand why when he says, "I could not feel any magic except yours."

I must not have heard him properly. "What?"

"Neither did I," Garren admits. No surprise there. He's often not in tune with what is going on. Maybe all the years he spent around the stench of the Dragons and the Goblins dulled his senses to everything else. The latter were particularly odiferous.

When Isla and Tana add that they were not able to sense the magic, either, I begin to get worried. Did I imagine it? I glance down at my unconscious Familiars. Nope, I did not imagine it. We were definitely fighting evil magic a few minutes ago. Unless I am still in some alternate reality and the Demons are playing a trick on me and it was really my own magic going haywire. Did the Demons somehow trick me into harming Taz and Felix with my magic? Panic begins to bubble inside me at the thought.

"I felt it." His voice is low and soothing, meant to calm my growing hysteria.

My eyes fly to Kallen. I search his face, his green eyes, for the truth in his words. I let my magical lie detecting skills do their thing. I sigh a great sigh of relief when I am certain he is telling the truth. He did feel it. He's not just placating me.

Isla is scowling. I think the idea of this being another reality altered by the Demons is going through her mind, as well. "How is it the two of you could feel the Demon magic when the rest of us could not?"

Fortunately, Kallen has a theory. Good thing, because I don't have a clue. "Exposure," he says simply. "Xandra and I spent every day in those other realities immersed in the magic. Perhaps we are more attune to it now."

Dagda nods. "It is a reasonable theory."

Tana concurs. "Dark magic, especially the darkest magic, is meant to be masked. I used spells myself that only the Familiars were able to sense." That's right, she did. Not that I like to be reminded of the days she wanted me dead, but sometimes useful tidbits of information arise from that time.

"I know this will not be a popular suggestion," Kallen begins and all eyes snap to him in dread. "But, I believe we need to return to the archives. Xandra and the rest of us need to be armed with as much information as possible if we are going to fight the Demons. I suspect if her Familiars had not been here, she would not have been as successful as she was in beating the Demon magic back." His eyes find Taz and Felix on the floor and I believe he has a new appreciation for my Familiars. "And they are not prepared to launch another counterattack any time soon."

"Maybe we shouldn't say that out loud," I gripe. "No sense in calling the Demons' attention to the fact that they are passed out on the kitchen floor."

Chagrined, Kallen nods. "You are right. I was assuming that they are watching us and would know this, but they may not be."

Watching us? He's right. They could be watching us right now like they made the others watch as Kallen and I struggled through the realities. A shiver runs down my spine. Demons watching us like we're on a reality show. Now, that's creepy. And if it's true, how long have they been watching us? I suspect that, unlike the Angels who could be watching at any given time, the Demons do not respect private moments. For that matter, was everyone watching Kallen and me when we made love in those other realities? I am definitely back to feeling nauseated again.

Thinking of Angels, my head whips around like I'm suddenly going to find a pair hiding in the corner of the kitchen. When I obviously don't find them, I ask the room in general, "Where are Raziel and Adriel?"

Isla's expression is grim. "I was wondering the same thing." Good thing she brought it earlier up, then.

"Have any of you seen them?" I ask. "Were they watching with you?"

"No. They have not been around for days," Garren says, confirming my worst fears.

My eyes fly back to Isla and her lips are pressed together. So tight, her nostrils are flaring a bit. She's not saying something. Something I suspect is important. "Spit it out," I demand through gritted teeth.

"Xandra, I do not know..."

Ire flashes through me and I inadvertently pull enough magic to make the house shake a little. "Tell me what you think has happened to them."

With a long suffering sigh, Isla says, "Angels and Demons are natural enemies. It is unlikely that the Demons would not take advantage of finding Fallen Angels in our midst."

I am going to punch her in the face if she doesn't just spit it out like I demanded a minute ago. Everyone here knows I am short on patience. Why do they make me pull information out of them so slowly that my precarious hold on my magic begins to slip? If it's because they think it will help me gain control they have seriously misguided hopes and dreams. "Meaning…" I growl.

Kallen puts a hand on my shoulder and squeezes gently. He finishes for Isla. "The Demons may have wanted to cause them greater harm than the rest of us."

I whirl to face him, knocking his hand away in the process. "Did you already figure that out and decided not to tell me?"

He is surprised enough by my accusation for me to know that he had not figured it out until Isla began speaking. "No," he hurries to say. "Honestly, I was so distracted by other events that I am only now realizing they are gone." His face turns an interesting shade of red when he realizes how awful it sounds that he just now figured out two friends are still missing.

I can't chastise him for it. I am only now asking about them myself. I should have done a roll call or something when we got home. Something I will definitely do during future catastrophes. I did briefly wonder where they were before Mom began sobbing in my arms, but then I was distracted. I am a terrible friend. "We need to figure out what happened to them. Before the Demons decide to kill them."

Tana, the never optimistic harbinger of doom, asks, "How can you be certain they are not already dead?"

Grabbing my arm before I can stalk across the room and slap her, Kallen scowls at his aunt. "Because the Demons are not stupid. Killing Angels, even Fallen Angels, would immediately start a war with the Angels. They are alive."

"Not to mention, they would want as much leverage as possible," Dagda adds. He moves closer to his wife because he's afraid he may need to defend her from me. Yeah, I wish him good luck with that if she continues to piss me off.

"I should check with the Angels." Maybe they can tell me where my friends are.

Kallen is the voice of reason. "I am certain they already know about the Demons. It is probably a better use of our time to revisit the archives right now."

I glower up at him. "Going to Angel time doesn't affect time in this reality," I point out snarkily.

"Demons and Angel have the same ability to move through time and space," Isla informs me.

Oh, so going to Angel time could be wasting precious time if the Demons experience time like I do. A sickening thought hits me. "If they can move in and out of Angel and realm time, does that mean they know the future like the Angels do?" If that's the case, maybe they attacked now because they already know they can win.

Isla shakes her head and my rising panic begins to ebb. "From what I understand, and mind you, my knowledge is limited, Demon abilities when it comes to such things is more akin to your ability than the Angels'." I may have just been insulted about my ineptitude there, but I am so relieved that the Demons don't know the future that I don't even care.

My relief is soon edged out by anger. "Wait a minute." I turn to Dagda. "Didn't the Demon say everything would be returned to normal?"

"I was having the same thought myself," he admits. "If a Demon must keep his word, why are they not present?"

I know why. "Because I was probably rash when deciding on the spur of the moment to trust a Demon," I chastise myself aloud. Might as well let everyone know I freely admit to what they are inevitably thinking.

"You did what was needed at the time," Dagda soothes.

Kallen wraps his arms around me. "We needed to be free of the other realities to focus on fighting the Demons. You accomplished that the best way you could at the time. Now, we can focus on rescuing our friends and vanquishing the Demons back to hell."

"In other words, you're saying I can't change what I already did, so let's go forward from here."

Kallen smiles at me indulgently. "You know me so well."

"Fine, then let's go to the archives," I concede. "I can't stand the idea that we left Raziel and Adriel in the hands of the Demons." Oh, what I am going to do to them if they are harming my friends. If the gruesome images of revenge running through my mind come true, I may need to consider that I have a little Demon blood running through my veins, as well.

A smile forms on Dagda's face. "I do not believe there is a need." He is staring through the window which looks out over the driveway. He moves to the door and opens it wide.

A second later, Tabitha comes trudging through with a large bundle of books in her arm. "Bring the rest in here," she calls over her shoulder.

I watch in amazement as several Fairies who must work at the palace follow her through the door with their own bundles of books. They pile them all on the kitchen counters, leaving the island counter free, and then go for more. There are seven piles in all when they are done.

As soon as they put the final books down, the two Fairies who helped Tabitha carry them from the carriage she used to get here stand by the door waiting for further instructions. Tabitha waves them away. "You can return to the palace. If the scribe has more, bring them immediately." With a nod to her and then the King and Queen, the Fairies turn and leave.

The rest of us stare open mouthed at the piles and piles of books. And scrolls. Some of them ancient and crumbling.

"They are only going to get read if you actually take them and open them," Tabitha snarks. "What are you waiting for? We have work to do."

20 CHAPTER

"I assume this is everything the scribe could find on Demonology?" Dagda says to Tabitha.

"No, they are recipe books," Tabitha mutters under her breath. This earns her a scowl from the King, but since she brought us all this information, saving us what would probably have been yet another dangerous trip to the archives with me involved, he can't really snark back.

"You must have started as soon as we left," I say, grabbing for a book. "Thank you."

Kallen reaches out and grabs my wrist, causing me to glare up at him in annoyance. "Tabitha, are any of these books from the dark magic section?" he asks. Good point. I probably shouldn't be grabbing any of these books until I know the answer to that question.

"Most of them," she informs us.

Trying to find a way not to sound offensive when he suggests I should not touch any of the books, Kallen's eyes find Taz and Felix. "Perhaps you should check on your Familiars. The rest of us can start on this."

Okay, he picked something more offensive to say. "I'm pretty sure they're just sleeping off the effects of the dark magic," I huff. "If I thought they were still in trouble, I would have done something about it already."

Kallen's eyes narrow. He struggles for a moment, but he manages to bite back the retort dying to jump off his tongue. I marvel at his restraint. "Of course," he says through teeth pressed together so tightly, his jaw hinges creak slightly. Loosening them only enough to be able to utter more words coherently, he says, "I was simply trying to keep you from killing yourself or others. But, by all means, pick any book you would like." I guess he couldn't hold back his snark, after all.

Well, if he's going to put it that way. I pull my hand back, folding my arms over my chest. "What do you expect me to do, not help?"

"Perhaps you and Tana could check the area," Dagda says innocently.

Not innocently enough for his wife. "My dear husband, do you suspect I will be tempted by the magic in these tomes?" Tana demands.

Maybe because I've already overreacted myself, I take pity on my father. I also sneak an 'I'm sorry' glance at Kallen as I say, "I don't think he's worried about you. I think, like Kallen, he's worried about the magic these books contain. They recognize something in us, and we don't want to give the magic a chance to escape. I was barely able to control them earlier today. I don't know if I'm up for a rematch yet." Actually, I feel like I could fight a thousand Demons I am so wound up. But, best I don't announce that to the masses.

After a look which promises Dagda that he and his wife will be having more words over this later, Tana turns and walks toward the door. I give Kallen a little smile and follow her outside. I figure at the moment, it's probably best to do the opposite of what the woman who once gave her soul over to evil does. Okay, that was harsh of me. Tana has been great lately. Still, it's easier to forgive than to forget.

"Do you want to stick together or split up?" I ask Tana. She is standing in the middle of the driveway with her arms crossed and her toe tapping. I suspect there are a lot of things on her mind, and whether or not we split up is not one of them. So glad I'm not a mind reader at the moment.

"What I want to know is when any of you will trust me." Her words are short and clipped, but there is pain in her eyes. Turns out, she is a lot less angry than hurt.

Guilt climbs up my brain stem. She has worked hard to prove to us that she has changed, yet we all still tip toe around her like she's one step away from psychoville. "It's not that Dagda doesn't trust you. He's worried for you," I try to clarify.

Tana is not having it. "Worried I will become evil again. That is the same as not trusting me." She does have a point.

I try a different tack. "Do you trust yourself one hundred percent to never fall prey to the pull of dark magic again?"

"Yes," the Fairy Queen responds without hesitation. Her eyes fixed squarely on mine, she adds, "I lost too much. I will never do anything to hurt those I love again."

I guess I didn't expect her to respond with such conviction. Which is why a dumbfounded response falls out of my mouth. "Really?"

Tana cocks her head to the side and gives me a sour look. "Thank you for letting me know where you stand in regards to trusting me." As my expression turns sheepish, hers softens. "I apologize. Of course you will always have a voice in the back of your head warning you to beware around me. That is my fault and I cannot expect it to go away simply because I have declared my ways changed."

By the end of her little speech, she appears so lost and heartbroken, I feel even worse. "No, you're wrong. I need to shut that little voice up. I know you're not going to turn evil again." I am tempted to hug her, but I'm not certain whether she would appreciate it or not. She ranks up there with Isla on not being a huge fan of the touchy-feelies.

Tana opens her mouth to respond, but my attention is caught by something else. A dark shadow has suddenly formed around the Fairy Queen. I have no idea where it came from, it just materialized. As I watch, it begins to take shape. Almost human shape. It swirls around her as if the being is made of smoke, but it definitely has arms and legs and a head. "Get away from her," I growl, startling Tana.

Panic in her eyes, Tana is instantly on high alert. "Xandra, what is it?" She whips her head around, looking for the danger she knows is in the air. But, she can't seem to see the Demon. Only I can for some reason.

I don't respond to Tana, my attention focused solely on the evil force surrounding her. I pull magic and prepare for a fight. Oh, how I wish Taz and Felix were out here with me. The Demon is making tighter and tighter circles as it slithers around Tana's body. Can't she feel it against her skin? "This is my last warning," I growl.

"Xandra, what are you going to do with all that magic?" Tana asks, fear making her voice louder and shriller than normal. Or, she's trying to get the attention of those inside.

"I am going to vanquish a Demon," I inform her evenly, not taking my eyes from the undulating evil.

"Are you certain there is a Demon present?" she asks. Her tone is taking on a pleading note.

"I can see it," I assure her.

The Demon turns its face toward me and smiles, exposing its charred gums and horrifying teeth. With a tongue like a lizard, it licks Tana's cheek. Tana doesn't even flinch. Gross. Why can't she feel that? "I can taste the evil that still resides in her," the Demon hisses. "She will make a perfect host."

Host? It's going to possess her?! "I won't let you have her," I snarl.

Tana's eyes are wide with fear now. "Xandra, what are you talking about? There is no one else here. It is only the two of us. Please, let the magic go."

I open my mouth to explain that she is wrong, that there is a Demon about to possess her. But, it happens so fast I don't have time. The Demon is slithering an inch from her body one second, and the next, it seems to mold itself to her form. In a flash, it sinks into her. "No!!" I cry and I let my magic fly.

Dagda's mournful shout rings through the air. "Xandra, no!"

It's too late, my magic has already made contact.

21 CHAPTER

The sheer horror in Dagda's voice snaps me back to my senses. I need to pull my magic back from Tana's convulsing form before I kill her. Yes, I need to exorcise the Demon from her, but it's not going to happen with blunt force magic, I'm sure. Before I can pull it back, though, I am tackled to the ground by my father. I don't believe he's trying to hurt me. He's trying to distract me. Hoping that if I turn my attention to him, I will forget about Tana. Unfortunately for him, my magic doesn't work that way. Now, it has two targets. It tears through Dagda just as it is Tana.

The driveway is filling with bodies. Kallen drops to his knees next to me, but he's smart enough not to touch me. "Xandra, what is going on?" His voice is calm, but there is an undertone of fear. Fear that I am about to kill two Fairies he loves.

I'm straining to pull my magic back so I need to force the words out. "Possessed. By. Demon."

I may have just shortened my husband's life by a few Cowan millennia. "You are possessed?" he asks as evenly as a terrified-that-his-wife-is-possessed-by-a-Demon husband can.

"No. Tana."

Relief flashes in Kallen's gorgeous green eyes. Which is quickly followed by guilt. He doesn't want his mother's sister to be possessed, either. His head swivels toward her and he stares hard. Then harder. "How do you know?"

"Saw it happen," I manage between gritted teeth. With a last tug, my magic comes rushing back to me so hard, I fall backwards. Both Tana's and Dagda's bodies are suddenly very still.

Tabitha rushes to Dagda, who happens to be closer to her. "He's alive," she announces.

"So is Tana," Isla calls out. "She is breathing."

Fortunately, Isla has not reached her yet. Scrambling to my feet, I cry, "Get away from her!" Did Isla not hear my conversation with Kallen? "She's possessed."

Isla stares back at me, doubt clouding the green of her eyes. "Possessed?" She takes a step back from Tana, but continues to stare at the Fairy lying unconscious on the ground. "Are you certain?"

I nod emphatically. "I saw the Demon meld with her."

Isla turns to Tabitha. "Check her, please."

Glancing between Isla and me, Tabitha asks, "Is it safe to touch her?"

"Perhaps it is best to take Xandra's word for it," Kallen suggests. "We know nothing of how Demon possessions work."

Dagda groans and pushes himself up on his elbows. "What happened?"

"Um, you got in the path of my magic," I admit. "Sorry about that."

Understanding washes over his face, followed by dread. His eyes begin a frantic search for his wife. When he finds her on the ground, he pushes himself up, ready to go to her. Kallen stops him with a hand on his shoulder. "Wait. I am not certain how much you heard, but we believe a Demon has possessed Tana."

Dagda shakes Kallen's hand off. "Nonsense. I sense no magic other than hers."

"Like you didn't sense the Demon magic these last few days," I point out.

An angry flush crawls up my father's neck. Whether he is angry at me or the Demons, I am not certain. "What can we do for her?" he demands of us all.

More than one shoulder wants to raise in a helpless shrug. I'm not embarrassed by my ignorance. I let mine do it. "I don't know."

"We cannot leave her out here on the ground," Dagda insists. "I will carry her inside." He marches forward, ready to pick his wife up in his arms and keep her safe.

He's about five feet away when Tana bucks her back and shoots to her feet like an acrobat. She could join the circus with skills like that. Her eyes are blazing with fury and it's all directed at me. "You!" She stalks toward me with homicide in her eyes. With an extra side of crazy. "You tried to kill me."

"Tana, you're possessed," I inform her. If Taz was out here, he'd mention how the Demon probably already knows this.

"Is that the excuse you gave them?" she mocks. "Everyone here knows you hate me and want me gone so your precious mother isn't uncomfortable."

Kallen comes to my defense. "Tana, that is not true. Xandra has never hated you."

"Like you would ever say anything to upset your sensitive little wife," Tana accuses.

"Hey! I'm not that sensitive," I exclaim, probably proving her point. Pulling myself together, I say as calmly as I can, "It's the Demon in you making you think these things. They are not true."

Tana gives me a 'you poor, stupid girl' look. "Demons cannot possess. Everyone here knows that."

"I do not know such a thing," Kallen counters.

"She is behaving strangely," Garren says in a stage whisper to Isla. "I believe Xandra is right."

Tana whips around so she is facing him and before Garren knows what hit him, he is on the ground. Wow, Demons are fast with their magic. Before Tana can strike again, though, I put a wall of my magic around her. I really hope it holds. I should also probably stop thinking of the Demon as Tana. She is still there somewhere, but it's pretty clear the Demon is the one in control.

I feel Kallen add his magic to mine. I glance up at him to give him an appreciative smile, but he's not looking at me. He's watching Dagda carefully. What is the King going to do now that we have his wife essentially caged in magic?

I'm not certain what he would have done if the Tana Demon remained calm and collected. But, when it hits the magic and lets out a bellow of rage so loud and insane it makes the trees tremble, what my father does is add his magic to mine and Kallen's. He moves closer to Kallen and me and I slip my hand in his, giving it a gentle squeeze in support of the difficult decision he just made. The right decision, but difficult all the same.

Inside the cage, the Demon's shrieks slowly become words, and they are some pretty nasty words. There is no way in any universe or reality that we could do the things with our body parts that it is suggesting. Some of them couldn't even be surgically accomplished by a coroner. Slowly, the words begin to change. They are in a language I don't understand, and I suspect that is not a good thing. Enough of that. I take its voice away.

As soon as the Demon realizes what I have done, it begins to rage again. Silent shouts and threats are directed toward me. It throws itself against the magic only to end up on the ground, writhing in pain. It hurts me to watch Tana's body be battered like this, but deep down, I am one hundred percent certain she would be angry if we let the Demon free. A quick glance at Dagda tells me he believes the same thing, though his hand does tighten significantly around mine. Ouch. I may need to get used to having only four fingers on that hand because there is definitely no circulation in my pinkie at the moment.

After a few minutes, Tana's body finally stops convulsing. The Demon is able to push up from the ground. It stands in the middle of the magical cage, careful not to touch any of the edges again. Its eyes glow an eerie silver and it snarls at me. Its expression is so angry and determined, I expect it to keep fighting against the magic. Oddly, it doesn't. It simply stands in the middle of the cage and glares at me. It's pretty creepy, actually.

"I believe being in Tana's body weakens the Demon," Kallen says quietly. "It cannot break through our magic in this state."

Interesting. A suspicion is niggling at my mind. Deciding to take a gamble, I approach the cage. "You, like your friend before you, are at our mercy," I inform the Demon residing within Tana. Unfortunately for us, like the position we were in with the last one, we cannot keep this up forever. "Unless you can free yourself of the body you have taken, you cannot fight us off. If I am wrong, get on with it so we can finish this fight. I really hate to kick someone when they're down." Unless it's a Demon. I find I could quite easily kick a Demon when it's down. If only it wasn't in Tana's body.

Out of the corner of his mouth, Kallen says, "Please do not antagonize the Demon."

I grin up at him. "Not antagonizing, just offering suggestions." I turn my attention back to Tana and her uninvited guest. "If you could leave her body on your own, I suspect you would have done it by now."

"Are you saying it is trapped within her forever?" Dagda asks. I have never heard his voice so anguished.

Keeping my eyes on the silver ones before me, I shake my head. "No, not forever. I am certain there is a spell or a ritual which can free the Demon. As a matter of fact, it began to speak one before I took its voice away."

Kallen's lips curl up into a grin as he stares down at me. "But you took its voice away before it could finish. You never cease to amaze me, my love."

I grin back. "That is what is going to keep us happily married for eternity."

He chuckles. "One of many things." The pure lust in his eyes gives me a clue as to another item on the list. I want nothing more than to kiss him at the moment.

"Can we please get back to saving my wife," Dagda hisses next to me.

Yes, we did get sidetracked. Addressing the Demon again, I say, "Your friend promised me that things would be back the way they were when his spell ended. He lied. I don't like liars." Something that really bothers me is that when the Demon lied, my internal lie detector didn't go off. Are Demons the one race of beings who I cannot read?

The Demon begins shaking its head. Well, Tana's head, and it's pointing at her mouth. Kallen scowls. "I believe the thing wants to speak to you."

Yeah, to say the exorcism spell. Since I didn't understand the Demon's language, nor do I know the spell, I have no idea how close it was to being finished, or if the spell must be spoken all at once or if it can be interrupted with a sudden loss of voice and picked up where the Demon left off when its voice returns. It might only have one or two more words and its done. Poof, it's gone and we lose the upper hand. I study the Tana Demon closely and wonder what to do about this stalemate. Nothing spectacular comes to mind. With a sigh, I reluctantly say to the Demon, "Here's the deal. If you utter one word that I don't understand, I will not only take your voice away, I will put Tana in a coma so you can't communicate or move at all. Do you understand?" Tana's head bobs up and down.

Isla and Garren move next to us. Both of them have had magic drawn since Kallen, Dagda and I caged Tana and the Demon. They draw more, ready to defend if the thing gets loose. Doing my best not to seem worried, I give the thing its voice back.

Doing a verbal check, the Demon lets out a piercing shriek. It's really hard not to cover my ears. I do not want to show any sign of weakness, though. Neither do the others around me. In fact, Kallen is giving the thing a rather dull stare as if bored with its theatrics. I really wish I could master facial expressions like he can.

But wow, I did not know that Tana's voice could reach those kinds of highs. She could have considered a career in the opera if she was from the Cowan realm. Not a great opera. Maybe a minor one in a small town somewhere. Her voice is high. She cannot necessarily carry a note.

"Do try not to damage her vocal cords. That will just piss me off more," I tell the Demon in as bored a voice as I can muster.

The thing quiets but its silver eyes flash bright in annoyance. I really hope Tana's eyes go back to green when the thing leaves her. The silver would be really hard to get used to. Not to mention make the whole 'I'm never going to be evil again' argument much more difficult to believe. Moving close to the magical wall but not touching it, Tana's lips curl back into a snarl. "You speak of liars when you live among races who do nothing but lie."

Shaking my head, I glance up at Kallen. "How many stupid comments do you think I should give it before I take its voice away again?"

With a smirk, Kallen replies, "One."

Nodding in agreement, I turn back to the Demon. "One it is, then. And you've used it up. Either say something useful or I take your voice and the rest of us go back inside. We have some important reading to do."

If the Demon isn't careful, it's going to saw Tana's tongue in half in its attempt not to say something stupid. At least it's taking me at my word. After a moment of what are probably evil enough thoughts to permanently damage Tana's brain waves, the Demon hisses, "You were given what you were promised."

I cock my head to the side. "Really?" I glance around as if looking for someone. "Because I seem to be missing some friends."

Tana's lips curl up into a demented smile. "Those you seek were gone before my brother's spell was cast. Angels are, after all, cowards."

I don't believe that for a second. I know my friends, and saying either of them is a coward is absolutely ridiculous. They would readily sacrifice themselves if they thought it would save the rest of us. A chill tickles my spine. Is that what they did? I will not give the Demon the satisfaction of asking. Suddenly pissed, I snarl, "If you are implying that Raziel and Adriel ran away because they were afraid of Demons, you won't get any of us to believe it." I tug on Kallen's hand as I turn around. "Let's go read some books," I say to my husband.

"They did not run away." There is both haste and great reluctance in the Demon's words. For some reason, it did not want to admit this, nor did it want to appear weak enough to not want me to go. Yet, it stayed my forward progress by admitting this. Interesting.

I throw a glare over my shoulder. "Then why aren't they here?"

The Demon takes so long to respond, I shake my head in disgust and turn back toward the house taking several steps, forcing its hand yet again. Finally, it hisses, "They were taken before the spell was cast."

Taken before the spell was cast? How is that possible? Raziel would have seen it coming. Then again, if it was inevitable that they were taken, he would have seen that coming, as well. He knows the future. He is not invincible.

Considering this Demon's words, I think back to how readily the first Demon agreed to my demand to have things returned to how they were before its spell was cast. It hits me how correct I was that my agreement with him would come back and bite me in the ass. The damn thing wanted to agree before I asked for something more specific like making sure all of my loved ones were accounted for and unharmed. Me and my stupid impatience. If I had done a little more probing, I may have been able to save Raziel and Adriel already.

"The thing is most likely lying," Kallen reminds me quietly.

A frustrated shriek erupts from Tana's lips. "Demons are incapable of lying!"

I turn to look at the caged being and smile wryly. "But, you do seem to have fantastic hearing."

"What do you mean, Demons are incapable of lying?" Kallen asks. He still sounds bored and uninterested. Good idea. Best not to sound too interested in what the Demon has to say.

"We were cast from the ashes of the Flames of Truth," the Demon declares as if we should all know this.

I shrug and readily admit my ignorance. I have so much of it in regards to the magical world still, there's no sense in trying to hide it. That gets me nowhere in situations like this. "Sorry, not up on my Demon lore."

"I believe it is telling the truth," Mom says from the kitchen doorway. I turn to find her holding a very old, leather bound book in her hand. She, Tabitha and Dad stayed inside to protect Zac and keep researching when Kallen, Dagda, Isla and Garren came out to face the Demon with me. Technically, they came out to see if I was crazy and attacking Tana. Fortunately, I'm not crazy and I was not attacking her. That would have made for very awkward family get-togethers in the future. "According to this, Demons were scraped together from the ashes of the Flames of Truth. The fire from which the Angels were created."

Okay, that I believe. In their true form, they definitely look like they were scraped together from some sort of ashes. But, that does not necessarily mean what the Demon is claiming is true. "Angels can lie," I point out to no one in particular. They're not supposed to, but they can. Belial is a perfect example. I'm pretty sure he lied all the time. Or, at least, came pretty darn close to it on many occasions.

"The flames were only one step in the process of creating the Angels," Isla explains. I believe she is implying that the other steps negated some part of the effect of the Flames of Truth. Definitely a question I will be asking my Angel friends in the future. Studying the Demon in the cage, she continues, "If these beings were created solely from those flames, it is possible they carry such a limitation which the Angels do not."

Quirking a brow, I ask, "Do you trust it?"

Isla's lip quirks up in an unamused half-smile. "Trust it? No. I believe it will twist the truth in a thousand different knots to mislead and confuse us."

"That was helpful," I complain under my breath. We might as well assume it can lie then.

Tired of being ignored, the Demon growls, "Do you not want to know what has befallen your friends?"

I give it an annoyed glance. "Let me guess, one of your buddies kidnapped them before your brother cast the spell. Now, they are being tortured mercilessly, and if we don't let you go, there is nothing we can do to stop it." Tana's expression turns surprised and I roll my eyes. "Obviously, you have never watched a Cowan horror movie. A variation of that is the plot of a good deal of them."

"What is she talking about?" Garren asks Isla. She shushes him. Now he's annoyed, but he has the good sense to keep quiet.

Spit shoots from Tana's mouth onto the driveway and the Demon hisses. Gross. If she's conscious inside there, Tana's probably horrified by such bad behavior. Then again, she is being possessed by a Demon. She may have bigger things on her mind than whether or not she just spit on the driveway. "I care nothing of Cowans," the Demon declares. "A waste of creation."

Wow. Cowans really are considered the scourge of the magical world. They really don't deserve such censure. The things they have been able to accomplish without the use of magic is pretty damn impressive. Could any of these other beings do the same? "My Dad and my brother carry Cowan blood. If you have any hope of convincing me to be anything but cruel to you, I would cut the anti-Cowan rhetoric."

"I will thrive on your cruelty," the Demon hisses with a smile that backs up its words.

Hmm, hadn't thought of that. Disturbing. Pulling my lips into my best smile, I reverse my position. "Then I will kill you with kindness." After a second of consideration, I correct that statement, too. "Or, I will simply kill you. I'm that determined to get my friends back." I didn't realize until this moment how true this statement is. I am faced with one of the darkest enemies I have ever come across. I suspect there is no cruelty beneath them, nothing they are not willing to inflict upon their enemies. Nor is there any moral argument which is likely to change their minds. Therefore, I will probably need to kill to get my friends back. Okay, I'm a bit nauseous now but I don't let it show. Instead, I harden my heart and face the very real possibility that I will be a murderer soon, even if it is in defense of family and friends.

The Demon must recognize something of its own darkness in my eyes because it believes me. "I will tell you how to get them back."

Cocking my head to the side, I stare at Kallen in disbelief. "Did the Demon just say that it is totally willing to betray its friends and family?"

Kallen nods. "It did. Worse yet, I believe it is serious."

Shaking my head, I intone to no one in particular, "They really are evil." Turning my attention back to the Demon, my voice is tinged with, okay, not tinged, *laden* with disgust. "You would have had me with 'I will let your step-mother go'," not really, but it doesn't know that, "but now that I know you are truly the lowest form of being in any universe and will totally rat out your friends to save your own ass, I plan to take full advantage of the fact. Before we get to that, though, tell me, are you harming Tana's body? Think carefully before you respond because if you are already harming it, it would not make a bit of difference if I harm it, as well." I hear Dagda hiss nearby, but he doesn't say anything. He knows me well enough to know I am bluffing. It is just the thought which bothers him, not that he believes I will actually do it. Hopefully, the Demon does not know this.

Whether out of fear of me, or simply because it cannot lie, the Demon replies, "The host body will eventually degrade, but the process takes centuries."

Hmm, time moves differently in each realm. "Cowan centuries or Fairy centuries?"

Annoyed to have been caught trying to mislead me, the Demon hisses, "Angel centuries."

Now I'm really confused. "Angel time doesn't move that way." It goes in and out of other realms' timelines.

Even more annoyed, the Demon admits, "It would take eons for her body to suffer the consequences of possession." Technically, it did not lie. Eons are made up of centuries. A lot of them, but still.

Although I am greatly relieved, I feign disappointment. "Then physically, you are safe. For now," I add with a malicious smile. "After all, Tana has never been my favorite Fairy in the universe."

Before I have the chance to say anything else which will definitely be the cause of my biological father's coronary, Kallen interrupts my back and forth with the Demon. "I believe it has been established that there will be consequences if you do not cooperate," he tells the Demon. "Where are the Angels?"

Tana's eyes shift from me to my gorgeous husband. "Hell," he says simply.

"There is no such thing as hell," Isla corrects. She glances at me. "At least, not as the Cowans know it." I believe her. We had this discussion when I was going to the Shadow realm.

"I will ask only one more time. Your lack of cooperation will mean your ultimate destruction," Kallen drawls. "Where are the Angels?"

"The place where the roots of all universes collide," the Demon says in a voice as bored sounding as Kallen's. You know, it's cute when Kallen does it. Freaking irritating as hell when a Demon does it.

"Great, I assume you can draw us a map." There is only a hint of sarcasm in my voice. Truly, I want a map to this god forsaken place. I assume it really is god forsaken. After all, which god would want to hang out with Demons? Well, there is Hades. Then again, he likes being the King of his underworld. I don't think he would let Demons intrude in his realm.

"A map?" The Demon is truly alarmed.

Scowling at Kallen, I ask, "Did it seem like an unreasonable request?"

Kallen shrugs. "A map would be most handy."

"I thought so." I turn my attention back to the Demon. "So, how soon can you draw that up?" To be helpful, Kallen creates a pad of paper and a pencil inside the cage. I smile up at him in appreciation.

Horrified by the suggestion, the Demon stutters, "A map?? A map cannot be drawn to this place."

Honestly, I suspected as much. Nothing is ever that easy when it comes to magical beings. Frowning, I still ask the obvious. "Why not? It exists, therefore directions can be given to find it." Out of the corner of my eye, I see Isla shift uncomfortably. She disagrees but she doesn't say this aloud.

"You need to be of Demon blood to find your way," the Demon hedges.

I smile broadly. "Great! You can bring us there."

Horror fills Tana's green and silver eyes. Yeah, I really hope those go back to normal. It's pretty freaky to see her like this. "I would be killed instantly," the Demon claims.

Again, I glance up at Kallen. "How is this our problem?" I ask sweetly.

He shakes his head. "It is not our problem," he assures me.

Desperation fills the Demon's words. "They would know I was coming. They would sense it. We would both be killed instantly."

A cocky grin covers my face. "I'm not quite that easy to kill. Trust me. Many of have tried." Wait, I'm not sure that's something to brag about.

Recovering some of its earlier confidence, the Demon forces Tana's lips into a malicious smile. "Even when faced with a hundred waiting Demons?"

Okay, that might be a problem. I am having enough trouble fighting them off one at a time. I don't believe I could fight off a hundred of them and survive.

Noticing my waning bravado, Kallen speaks up again. "If you had a hundred Demons waiting for us, they would be here rescuing you. Your numbers are not quite as great as that.

I open my mouth to correct him. Demons can't lie. Then, I consider what the Demon actually said. *Even when faced with a hundred waiting Demons?* A question, not a statement of fact. He was not saying there would be a hundred Demons waiting for us. He was simply trying to make me believe there would be a hundred Demons waiting for us. Tricky. I give Kallen's hand an appreciative squeeze for bringing this to my attention. He smiles down at me adoringly. Lord, he is sexy when he is adoring me.

Bringing my attention back to the problem at hand, I ask the Demon point blank, "How many of you are there?"

"One," he answers readily.

Okay, I need to be more specific. "How many Demons are still alive and want to kill, torture, maim, cast spells upon, observe and generally annoy us?"

The Demon takes a moment to consider my question. I can see Tana's brain ticking off the qualifications as the thing considers its brethren. It is also trying to find a way to answer my question in a way which does not betray an actual number. This alone tells me that there are not many of them. My heart swells at the prospect of only a handful of Demons to fight instead of a hundred.

As usual, my hopes are always dashed. At least, somewhat. "Twenty," the Demon finally admits. Yet, it is much less crestfallen with this admittance than I would have thought. There is a glint in Tana's now completely silver eyes which tells me I have once again been tricked into believing something that is not one hundred percent true.

My mind is racing trying to come up with a better question. It is Kallen who thinks of one first. "How many of these twenty are actually a threat to us?" Wow, I never would have thought of that. Are some of the Demons too old or feeble to fight? Or too young? Maybe some never recovered from the war or whatever that killed the rest of them off. That would explain why they haven't shown up until now.

The Demon is quiet for so long, I once again turn back toward the house. I could be reading a book instead of waiting for it to speak. A much better use of my time. Kallen and I are at the kitchen door when the Demon says, "Seven. There can only be The Seven."

My mind begins to tick off the clues the Demon has given us. Flames of Truth, the place where all universes collide, the need for Demon blood and that there can only be seven. These things will definitely narrow our research a bit. Mom is no longer at the door, but I bet she can still hear what is being said. Hopefully, she and Tabitha have already begun a new search with these clues in mind.

Assessing the Demon for a long moment, I cock my head to the side. "How close were you to finishing the spell to un-possess Tana?"

A frustrated growls escapes Tana's lips. "Very close."

I roll my eyes. "How many words away?"

To my surprise, the Demon stops to count. "Thirteen," the thing admits.

Thirteen? Really? How ironic. "What happens if you are forcibly removed by someone else?"

A wicked smile curves Tana's lips. "Both the host and I will die." There is no way to misinterpret that. Nor the triumphant gleam in its eyes. The Demon is telling the truth. Crap.

22 CHAPTER

"Xandra!" Mom calls from the door. "There are some things you should see."

Good. I really need to get out of this Demon's presence for a few minutes as I'm starting to get frustrated and impatient again. Never a good combination for me. Turning back to the Demon, I smile, "Not that I don't trust you…wait, I don't trust you." I pull more magic and take Tana's voice away. Can't have the thing saying those last thirteen words to complete the spell. For right now, it's best to keep the Demon inside Tana's body. I see the hurt in Dagda's eyes, but I harden my heart to it. I would like to think I would do the same thing if it was Kallen in the cage possessed by a Demon. Really, I would.

All of us pile back into the kitchen. Dagda is the last to join us, reluctant to leave his wife to the mercy of the

Demon, but he does join us. Kallen reaches out and puts a hand on his shoulder. "It will not hurt her. It is smarter than that," he assures the Fairy who is both his father-in-law and his uncle by marriage. There is a lot of love between the two despite the fact that there is no shared blood between them. He knows Kallen has his best interest at heart.

Still, Dagda remains unconvinced. "We shall see."

We should probably change the subject before he goes mad. Turning to Mom and Tabitha, I ask, "What did you find?"

Pointing to several books left open on the kitchen island counter, Mom replies, "Several things." She moves closer and pulls one of the books to her. "First, I happened to be reading this when the Demon said there could only be seven. Another thing it is telling the truth about."

Isla and Garren move next to her. "Seven Demons?" Garren asks. "How can that be if the thing said there are at least twenty of them."

Mom shakes her head. "Not seven Demons. Seven *active* Demons," she clarifies.

Brow scrunched, Kallen asks, "What do you mean by active?"

"It has to do with why the Demons were almost completely destroyed." Mom spins the book around so Kallen and I can read it better, much to the annoyance of Isla and Garren. "Only seven Demons control the collective magic of the whole. The others basically serve as power sources. They can't wield any magic on their own. The Angels were able to find most of them and destroy them before The Seven fought them back."

Shaking my head, I declare, "That's asinine. Why would the power of an entire race be controlled by seven? It seems like the others would rebel at some point."

Mom shakes her head in contradiction. "They are created to serve. That's all the others do and they accept their fate, apparently. They gladly serve by propagating then allowing the rest of their energy to be zapped by The Seven."

"Eew," I grimace. "Did you need to mention the propagating part? I could have gone the rest of my life without thinking about Demon sex."

"Trying to be informative," Mom grumbles, her cheeks turning pink. That's a nice thing about her not being a ghost anymore. She now blushes as often as I do.

"It is appreciated," Isla tells her with a censuring look in my direction. Fine, I won't complain anymore about images of Demon sex etched into my brain. Great, there's another one simply because I thought about it again. Eew.

"How do they take the energy from the others?" Kallen asks, trying to get off the topic of Demon sex. I suspect he has some unwanted images in his mind, as well. Good. We're married, we should share in the pleasant and the disgusting.

Reading through the passage, which is upside down for her, Isla is the one to respond. "It does not say." She turns the page, hoping for more information, but is disappointed by the fact that there isn't any. She closes the book in disgust. A little too hard because a bunch of dust goes flying into the air causing her to sneeze. It has obviously been a while since someone perused this book.

"You said you found other information?" Kallen says to Mom.

Mom nods and I can tell that despite the circumstances, she loves that she can be helpful in this type of way. A physical way, even if it is the simple act of scouring books and doing research. As a ghost, her assistance was limited in scope. She wouldn't even have been able to turn the pages herself. She directs our attention to an ancient looking scroll and biting her bottom lip, another trait I come by honestly, she says, "A prophecy of sorts. At least, I think that's what it is. I can't really tell."

I groan aloud. "I really hate prophecies," I complain.

Kallen winks at me. "The prophecy about you turned out better than expected."

I'm tempted to stick my tongue out at him. I'm too old and mature for that now, though. I need to come up with an older and more mature alternative, but I can't think of one right now. "Yes, after millennia of people worried sick over it. That's why prophecies suck. No one understands them until after they happen."

"They do tend to be tricky," Isla admits distractedly. She is busy reading the current prophecy we need to worry about.

"What does it say?" Garren asks, his impatience rivalling mine.

Her brows bunched together, Isla shakes her head. "It cannot be."

I'm ready to rip the scroll out of her hands. The only thing keeping me from doing this is the fact that the scroll will probably crumble into a pile of dust if I do. Even Kallen is growing impatient with her, and sometimes I wonder if he really knows the definition of the word. Okay, that's a stretch. He's often impatient with me and my antics. Can't say I blame him half the time. The other half, I definitely blame him. "Grandmother," he says between gritted teeth, "please either read the prophecy aloud or pass the scroll so I may read it to everyone."

With a sour look in her grandson's direction, Isla decides to read it herself. *"Through generations the seed is planted. A crime never to be descanted. Until the day knowledge is needed, complete discretion to be heeded. Blood diluted yet magic strong, inside lurks the Demon song. A weapon made frail and delicate, the wielder feared morally desolate. The champion of good must take up the fight, for the dark beacon will call them to the light. The only way for hope to prevail, tis this the universe's last countervail."*

"And that is why I hate prophecies," I complain. "That makes no sense."

Placing the scroll on the counter, Isla uses one finger to point at the bottom. "Look to whom this particular prophecy is attributed."

This cannot be good. Leaning closer, I stare at the place her finger is indicating. I stare harder. I'm hoping that my eyes are simply not functioning correctly. Next to me, Kallen curses under his breath. "He is such a wanker," he mutters. I admit, this time I agree.

"I could not believe it myself," Tabitha complains bitterly. "He knew this was coming, and he had vital information to share. Yet, he let himself and Adriel be taken by those vile creatures."

Okay, I loathe to do it, but I feel like I must defend my friend. "It's against Angel law to tell us," I remind her.

Tabitha cocks her head and gives me a look of reproach. It makes me glad I'm not within smacking distance or the back of my head would be sore about now. "Would you keep Angel law in mind if Kallen was going to be kidnapped and tortured by Demons?"

What a stupid question. Of course I wouldn't. Which is why Raziel is a much better Angel than I am. "I'm only part Angel," I say feebly. "He's an Archangel. He has more to lose than I do."

Getting on the 'defend Raziel' bandwagon, Mom says, "He did leave us a clue." Touching the ancient scroll, she adds, "Centuries ago, apparently."

"Don't care how long ago, the bloody Angel still left us at the mercy of Demons," a voice complains bitterly from the floor. To my surprise, it is Felix who utters these words. He actually likes Raziel. A quick glance at Taz tells me he is rousing, but not quite awake enough for speech yet. Probably a good thing. He would have a lot more colorful things to add to the conversation. None of them happy, joyful words.

"Perhaps we should worry less about when or why he left us this clue, and focus more on how we can use it to save my wife," Dagda growls. He's been so quiet, I almost forgot he was here.

"He is right," Kallen agrees, nodding his head in apology to the King.

We all turn our eyes back to the scroll. Great. Deciphering prophecies, my least favorite thing in the world. "I guess we start at the beginning," I say. I wait for Taz to make a snarky comment about me stating the obvious, but he must be too groggy still. I glance over my shoulder at him just to make sure he's alright.

"Do no worry, I am certain he will be back to making disparaging comments in no time," Felix assures me from his friend's side. I smile at him. Taz is in good hands. I turn back around and it belatedly dawns on me that Felix knew Taz would make a disparaging remark about what I said. Something tells me that Felix may sometimes be thinking what Taz is saying aloud. Hmm. Not sure if I like that idea. My perception of Felix is suddenly skewed. Nah, I'm thinking too hard about nothing. I hope.

Kallen reads the first line again. "'Through generations the seed is planted.' It seems a direct reference to Xandra."

A deep frown etched on her face, Isla says, "That makes sense. Several things had to line up genetically for Xandra to be created." If she believes Kallen is right, why is she scowling?

"You make me sound like Frankenstein's monster," I complain. I get several dull stares and a sympathetic pat on the back from Mom, the only one to get the reference.

"You are not a monster," Mom assures me.

"Gee, thanks," I snark under my breath.

Ignoring me, Isla continues. "Except the next line. 'A crime never to be descanted.' Xandra's impending birth was discussed ad nauseam beforehand."

"Again, feeling the love," I grumble. This time, Isla gives me a sour look for my comment.

"Maybe he meant the fact that her destiny changed. She was never supposed to figure that out," Kallen suggests, but his tone implies even he doesn't believe this.

Neither agreeing nor disagreeing with Kallen, Dagda moves closer to read the next lines. "'Until the day knowledge is needed, complete discretion to be heeded.'

A useless turn of phrase. He is simply stating he will not risk his wings unless absolutely necessary." Wow, cynical much?

"Hey, that's a good point," I say thoughtfully. "Raziel created this prophecy to give us clues *before* something is resolved. He very well could lose his wings for this." Guilt washes over me. Was he so certain of my failure without his assistance that he felt he needed to sacrifice himself? Not feeling very confident at the moment. On the other hand, he must have foreseen success with these clues. Okay, I got this. I hope.

Kallen reaches over and gives my hand a squeeze. "I should not have called him a wanker. It appears he is still a good friend."

Dagda snorts. "If he is going to lose his wings for this, why not simply tell us and avoid all this pain?"

"He may have received permission to create the prophecy," Isla says somberly, taking away all the perceived heroics of Raziel's actions. "As it is simply a series of clues as opposed to a statement of what is to come. After all, the Angels and Demons have always hated one another. Perhaps they deemed this a case where interference was necessary for both our and their own survival. They have done such things before."

"Wankers will do what wankers do," Taz grumbles. Despite his words, I turn and smile at him. I'm glad he's awake and aware again.

Wanting to get off the subject of whether or not Raziel is a wanker, I move on to the next part. "'Blood diluted but magic strong.' That definitely sounds like me. I have a little bit of three different beings in my genetic makeup."

Without looking up from the scroll, Dagda intones, "Four if this is to be believed." Despite the lack of inflection in his voice, his words hit me hard.

"You think I have Demon blood in me?" I gasp. I know I sometimes have some pretty evil thoughts, but this is a bit much.

Kallen's hold on my hand grows tighter. "I do not believe it."

I appreciate my husband's undying faith in me and my bloodline, but I seriously doubt Raziel would lie. "What else could that mean, then?"

Not ready to back down from his stance, Kallen points out, "It reads that you have the Demon song within you, not Demon blood. Which could simply mean that you know how to fight them."

"I am not convinced this is about you at all." Every eye in the room flashes to the speaker of those words. Garren flinches at the onslaught.

"Explain," Isla commands in her best High Chancellor voice.

Squaring his shoulders, Garren visibly chafes at her imperial tone but explains anyway. "The very next line indicates it is not Xandra."

As if choreographed, all eyes move from Garren back to the scroll. We read the next line. *A weapon made frail and delicate.* Okay, he has a point. Frail and delicate have never been words used to describe me. "Unless…Maybe he meant before I came into my magic," I suggest, not really believing it.

"That could be," Isla agrees, but she isn't convinced either. I believe she is leaning more toward Garren's suggestion. Wow. Wouldn't it be crazy if he was the one to figure all of this out? He's not exactly known for his analytical prowess. Look at me being all judgmental like it really matters who solves this as long as it gets solved.

Ignoring the part about the wielder being morally desolate, I skip to the next part. "But aren't I the champion of good? The first Demon said that this was all happening because there was too much of a shift in the universe toward good."

Kallen doesn't comment on this. He is already on to the next part. "What is this dark beacon? It seems to be responsible for calling the Demons to us."

"Am I the dark beacon?" I wonder aloud. After all, this prophecy is indicating that I have Demon blood coursing through my veins.

"Not everything is about you," Taz grumbles, pushing himself to a standing position. "Your vanity could fill the ocean and still need space to comb its hair."

"I am not quite that vain," I drawl. "And if you are so doubtful it's about me, what's your idea?" I challenge.

Waddling over to me, Taz stares up at me with mocking eyes. "Maybe you should take a nap, your brain might work better, more like mine."

"Is that your great idea?" I counter snarkily.

"Keelan, you moron. It's Keelan."

My heart stutters. It sputters. It comes grinding to a halt for several long seconds. It can't be. The fact I am even considering that he is correct must mean my brain is not getting enough oxygen. Keelan? Really.

Grasping my shoulders gently, Kallen asks, "What is it? What have you figured out?"

I feel my head shaking slowly from side to side of its own volition. "Not me. Taz."

Brows drawn in doubt that Taz could have solved the mystery, Kallen glances down at my Familiar. "Okay, what has Taz figured out?"

Taking a deep breath to be certain my brain is getting some oxygen, I spit out, "Keelan."

There are a few gasps around the room. Specifically, from Mom, Tabitha and Garren. Dagda and Kallen are blank faced as they absorb my words. Isla, on the other hand, suspiciously looks like she may have already come to this very same conclusion. "You knew?" I accuse.

Kallen's eyes follow mine and he sees what I see. "Grandmother? You believe this to be true?"

With a long suffering sigh, Isla admits, "The idea was forming in my mind before Xandra had her discussion with the Tasmanian devil."

"It fits." Dagda's voice holds no doubt. "It is too much of a coincidence for the Demons to have shown up on the night of his birth for it not to be him."

I really don't want it to be true for so many reasons. The primary reason being Alita and Kegan. How in the hell do we tell them that their baby is part Demon? Not to mention, how am I supposed to use a baby as a weapon? The words morally desolate from the prophecy come back to haunt me. I would be morally desolate to do such a thing. It's unfathomable.

"Alita's ability to detect dark magic," Kallen says thoughtfully.

Isla responds to his unasked question. "It could stem from Demon lineage."

"Wouldn't one of her parents show some indication that they have Demon blood within them?" I ask.

"Not necessarily. Not if the lineage comes through her mother," Kallen says thoughtfully. "As a Cowan, her mother has no magical abilities whatsoever. Perhaps it is the magic in Alita's Fairy blood which activated the latent ability in her family line."

"And the boost of Kegan's strong magic gave Keelan an even bigger push," I add. His reasoning seems sound even if I don't like it.

"That would explain why the babe was so powerful in utero," Tabitha adds.

"Okay, say I believe this craziness," I begin, earning me several annoyed looks. "What good does it do us? There is no chance I'm going to in any way use Keelan to fight the Demons. I mean, look at what happened here just half an hour ago. Taz and Felix almost died when I used them to fight off just one Demon. Now we know there are seven of them I need to fight."

"Six," Mom interrupts.

"What?"

"The first Demon you came across, you made it promise to never come after you again," she reminds me.

Kallen shakes his head. "I do not believe that is how it works." He is once again looking at the passage in the large tome which discussed The Seven Demons. "I believe that Demon will simply be absorbed back into the fold and another will come forward. If I am reading this correctly, there will always be seven."

"Just when I get my hopes up things might be the slightest bit easier, you stomp all over my dreams," I mutter.

His lips curved into a half smile, Kallen says, "Sorry, my love. I will try not to stomp on any more of your dreams in the future."

I smile back. "Much appreciated."

"If we could stay on topic," Dagda drawls. "I would like to remove that thing from my wife sooner as opposed to later, and we seem to have the answer now."

I try not to snap at him. I understand he is in pain, but as far as I can see, we aren't any closer to his goal than we were when we came back into the house. "Then we need to think of something that does not involve Keelan. There is no way I am going to use him."

Meeting my annoyed glare with his own, Dagda says, "I am not suggesting you do anything which will harm the boy."

I jab a finger toward my Familiars. "You saw what happened to them."

"They do not carry Demon blood in their veins," Dagda counters.

"And we don't know for certain that Keelan does, either, do we?"

"How do we determine if he does?" Kallen interrupts.

My mouth drops open as I stare at my husband in disbelief. "Are you suggesting I use a baby to fight my battles?"

Scowling, Kallen's words are terse. "I am not suggesting you bring a baby into battle, no. I am suggesting that there may be power in his blood. If this is the case, there may be a spell you could use to activate the power."

Oh, that seems reasonable. If all I need is a drop or two of blood for a spell, that wouldn't be so bad. Yet, the words morally desolate from the prophecy come back to haunt me again. I think it unlikely I will get off that easily or Raziel would not have used such a phrase. But, I'm going to try to be optimistic. "Okay. So, who is going to tell Kegan and Alita that their baby is part Demon? And Alita, too, for that matter." Alita already struggles with self-esteem issues. This is not going to make them better.

"I believe it is time Alita and Kegan came home," Isla says matter-of-factly. "Kallen, send them a message."

"What?! No." All eyes turn to me and I rush to remind them all, "Alita can't be around dark magic, remember?"

Kallen reaches over and squeezes my hand. "There is no dark magic for her to react to right now. And if the Demons do attack, there is no guarantee she is any safer with her parents."

I narrow my eyes at him. "You were just as insistent as me about them staying put earlier."

Lips pressed in a grim line, Kallen nods once. "That was before we had all the facts. My love, if Keelan really is the beacon who called the Demons, whether we use him as a weapon or not, his life is danger. We need to protect him and I do not believe leaving him in a cottage with three of the least powerful beings in this realm is the way to do it. Even with Kegan there, they as a group will provide little resistance if attacked."

Now that he has put it that way, I feel really stupid. Of course Keelan is in danger. But, before I can open my mouth to agree we should bring them home immediately, Dagda cuts me off. "Xandra, please be reasonable…"

I hold my hand up to cut him off. "Before you say something that totally pisses me off and we get into an argument where I do something stupid or dangerous to you when we have other things to be focusing on, I am going to get Kegan, Alita and Keelan." Look at me being all self-aware.

"Shouldn't Alita's parents come, as well?" Mom asks.

I nod. "They can hang out with Dad and Zac. I'll make two trips." Standing on my toes, I give Kallen a quick kiss. "I'll be back in a minute." I teleport myself back to the beach debating how much I tell Kegan and Alita before bringing them home. I'm pretty sure I'm going to take the coward's way out and wait until we can tell them as a group. See, I'm becoming even more self-aware.

23 Chapter

The cottage is so quiet when I arrive, for a second I fear I am too late. I am relieved when I feel magic behind the door. Before Kegan can whip the door open and attack first, discover my identity later, I call out, "It's me!"

The door opens a crack and I see one of Kegan's green eyes. "It looks and feels like you, but how can I be certain you're not a Demon?"

Oh, good question. Um. "I don't know," I admit.

To my surprise, Kegan opens the door completely and steps outside with me. "I suspect a Demon would have had a better reply than that." Good point.

"Yeah, I'm not up on my supervillain excuses."

"Why are you back here?" Concern washes over his face. "Is someone hurt? Do you need my help?"

"No and sort of," I hedge. "Actually, I came to bring all of you home."

Crossing his arms over his chest, Kegan gives me a hard stare. "I'm considering the idea that you might be a Demon again. After all, it was you and my cousin who insisted this is the safest place for my family to be."

"We've uncovered some things which make that less true now."

Of course Kegan's not going to let that vague as hell statement stand. "What, exactly, have you uncovered?"

"We'll explain at the house," I stall.

Shaking his head, Kegan says, "Uh uh, you will explain now or we are not going anywhere."

I'm tempted to reach out and simply teleport him back to the house, but I try not to use my magic against the people I care about. Instead, I need to gather my courage and tell him. So, in my usual blunt style I blurt it out instead of easing into it. "Alita has Demon blood in her family tree and Keelan is the reason the Demons are here."

To my surprise, Kegan doesn't say anything. I take a step closer, assessing him for shock. He looks fine, though. He's not pale, his skin isn't sweaty or pasty. His eyes aren't dilated and he doesn't appear dizzy or queasy. "Um, did you hear me?" I ask.

Kegan nods. "I did. Since what you said is too ridiculous to be true, I am simply waiting for you to tell me why you are really here demanding my family return to Grandmother's with you."

He doesn't believe me. Considering the fact that I don't really believe it myself, I can't blame him. "I know it's a lot to take in, and I don't even know for certain if it's true or not," I admit. "But, if there's even the slightest possibility that Keelan is in danger, we need to protect him."

His eyes flashing with anger, Kegan growls. "I am protecting him."

I put my hands up, palms forward. "I didn't mean to insult you or insinuate that you're not protecting him. The rest of us simply want to help protect him. And we can do that better if we're all together," I insist.

I receive a full minute of Kegan glaring at me, probably deciding the best way to dismember my body after he kills me considering the crazy glint in the corner of his eye, before he finally says something. "We will accompany you back to the house simply so I can laugh in your collective faces when it is proven my sweet wife and innocent child have no blood flowing through their veins other than Fairy and Cowan."

I nod. "Fair enough. I will teleport you in two trips."

This takes him by surprise. "You want to separate Alita and me?" he asks suspiciously.

"No," I assure him. "I will take the three of you first and then come back for her parents. We don't want to leave them unprotected, either."

Scowling now, Kegan reminds me, "They were safe here during the first Demon attack."

"I know, but that doesn't guarantee their continued safety. They will be keeping my dad and Zac company while the rest of us figure out how to stop the Demons." I mention my dad and Zac to put Kegan's mind at ease. He knows I will die before I let anything happen to either of them.

With a curt nod, Kegan turns back toward the door. "Come on."

I follow him inside. Alita and her parents are sitting at the kitchen table enjoying a cup of tea. Alita smiles when she sees me, but it is forced. She knows my return cannot possibly be a good thing. I always love being the harbinger of doom.

"Things have gotten worse," Alita says softly. Not a question.

I glance at Kegan and he shakes his head slightly. Yeah, like I was just going to blurt out, 'well, if you being part Demon is worse, then yup, things got worse.' Okay, I did sort of do that outside. He's probably right to warn me away from the topic. But, she does need to know sooner as opposed to later. I raise my brow in question. When should she find out?

Kegan answers my unasked question. "There is a theory the others have and they need us to weigh in on it. We are all going to Grandmother's house."

"All of us?" Alita's mother asks in surprise.

I nod. "We really want to make sure you're safe."

Instead of replying to me, Alita's father defers to Kegan. "Do you believe this is for the best?"

Kegan nods. "I do. Xandra is going to teleport us." Turning to his wife, he asks, "Is there anything you would like to bring?"

Alita shakes her head. "No, when Raziel insisted Keelan and I come here in the middle of the night, we did not have time to grab anything."

My jaw comes completely unhinged. How else can I explain the loud thump of it hitting the floor? "What?"

Kegan explains. "Right before the Demons cast their spell, Raziel and Adriel got Alita and Keelan to safety. I thought they would have told you that already."

"They're missing," I blurt. I slap a hand against my mouth before any more stupidity falls out of it. I had not meant to worry them yet.

"Missing?" Alita gasps.

"Okay, I need to get you guys home where everything can be explained by someone much better at it than me," I declare.

Alita stands up and reaches her arms out toward her mother who is currently holding Keelan. The baby's grandmother relinquishes the child, but there is reluctance in her eyes. She suspects all is not well in the realm. She is one perceptive, possibly Demon-infused Cowan. Once Keelan is safely in her arms, Alita walks to Kegan. "We are ready," she announces stoically even though she is obviously far from ready.

Reaching out, I pull her into a quick hug. "Everything will be fine," I assure her.

Alita nods. "It always is." Sure would have been nice if there was some oomph behind her words.

24 CHAPTER

I teleport Alita, Kegan and Keelan to the beach in front of the house. Too crowded in the kitchen to teleport so many of us directly there, and I don't want to risk causing Alita to drop the baby. I also don't want them to see Tana trapped in magic on the other side of the house quite yet, hence depositing them on the opposite side of the house from where everyone is assembled. There is so much for them to learn. Might as well shock their system with an overload of information all at once than bombard them with it one piece at a time. Though, either way is going to suck.

"I'll be right back," I say before teleporting back to the cottage. I grab Alita's parents and am back home before Kegan and Alita have entered the house.

"Where would you like us?" Alita's father asks.

Biting my bottom lip, I debate how rude it is to send them off without giving them all the pertinent information. I guess not as rude as I think because Kegan says, "I believe Xandra mentioned keeping you safe with her father and brother. Are they upstairs?" He gives me a pointed look telling me I better respond in the positive. He isn't ready to share the Demon-infusion theory with his in-laws yet. Can't say I blame him. I didn't want to share it with him.

"Yes," I nod. "They are in the sitting room on the second floor. Do you know where that is?" I hope so. I don't want to waste the time showing them. Wow, I really am rude. That's really not new information, though.

"Yes, of course," Alita's father assures me. Makes sense. They've been guests here many times over the years.

Inside the house, we part ways. Alita's parents make their way upstairs while the rest of us go to the kitchen. There, we find a bunch of somber faces. At least, until the baby enters the room. Then, there is a lot of gushing and oohing and aahing which tries hard to mask the somber faces. It barely works. It's really hard to be truly excited when you are about to tell the child's mother he is the only weapon available to fight off seven Demons. It's been a while since I mentioned this, but our lives can really suck sometimes.

After Keelan makes the rounds and ends up in his great-grandmother's arms, Isla clears her throat. "We have some information we must share. Alita, Kegan, perhaps it is best if you take a seat."

"Xandra already spoiled the surprise," Kegan says, crossing his arms over his chest. "And I do not believe a word of it."

"Believe what?" Alita asks.

"Believe that you carry Demon blood in your veins."

"It is true?" Alita gasps, clasping a hand over her mouth. She seems to be surprised and horrified, but not altogether shocked by the information. Okay, maybe I need to sit down because this is not the reaction I expected. Glancing around the room, I see I am not the only one eying a stool.

"You knew?" Kallen asks.

Alita's pale green eyes are locked onto Kegan's. No one in the room is quite as surprised as her husband at the moment. The shock I expected from him earlier has come on with a vengeance. His pupils are dilated, his skin has instantly acquired a sweaty, pasty appearance and he may have stopped breathing.

Kallen reaches out and steers Kegan toward the nearest stool. "You should sit down."

"I never believed it," Alita says miserably. "Mom told me the story when I was young, but I thought it was simply a story parents tell their daughter to scare her into being a good girl. I never thought she was telling me the truth."

"Perhaps you should enlighten us. What story did she tell you?" Isla asks as kindly and patiently as her raging curiosity will allow. Which means she sounds pushy and demanding.

"Yes, please tell us the story of how my wife and child are part Demon," Kegan insists roughly. I have never seen him angry with Alita before. I am going to assume it is because she kept this from him, not because he is going to love her any less with Demon blood running through her veins. I know I would love Kallen just as much. He could have toad blood running through his veins and croak every third word he says and I would still love him just as much. I would probably keep our conversations a little briefer, though.

Alita sends Kegan a pleading look, begging him to still love her despite her possible heritage. Not being a fool, at least not *always* being a fool, Kegan's features soften and he moves closer to his wife, hugging her close. "Tell us the story," he says in a kinder tone.

Her courage reinforced by his actions, Alita begins to speak. Her eyes remain steadfastly on Kegan, but the tale if for all of us. "It was Black Donald."

I snort. Really, I can't help it. "Black Donald? The Demon's name was Black Donald?"

Isla remarks coolly, "The less we interrupt, the sooner we will have the story." Fine. I make a buttoning of my lips motion with my hand and indicate that Alita should continue.

Taking a deep breath, Alita says, "One of my mother's great-grandmothers was a Scottish lass with more fire in her loins than brains in her head. At least, that was family legend." Her cheeks color at such a description of a member of her own family. Next to me, Kallen needs to cover a snicker with a cough and Kegan is no better. This time, they are the ones getting the censuring looks. Ah, vindication.

"So, she lay with a Demon?" Dagda asks, hoping to hurry the story along.

Alita shakes her head. "No, she turned him down flat."

Nonplussed like the rest of us, Kallen asks, "Then why do you believe you carry Demon blood in your lineage?"

"She is not telling the story correctly," a soft voice says from the doorway. We turn to find Alita's mother standing there. Apparently, she didn't like the idea of being stuck away upstairs. Can't say I blame her.

Relief passes over Alita's features. "Mother, will you please tell the story?"

Coming farther into the room, her mother nods. "I do not know how familiar you are with Scottish Cowan lore," she says, glancing around the room.

"Not at all," Dagda informs her, not unkindly but with a sense of urgency for her to get the tale told.

Taking the hint, Alita's mother begins speaking and no one interrupts until her tale is finished. "In Scottish lore, Black Donald is the devil himself. He tries to hide his identity when dealing with Cowans, but he has cloven feet which cannot be shod, therefore exposing him wherever he goes to those who are observant." Yes, I would probably notice a fellow's cloven feet.

"The Cowans try hard to appease Black Donald for fear that he will destroy their crops and ruin their lives." I try to hide a smile. It has been a long time since Alita's mother was in the Cowan realm, centuries by their measure of time. A lot has changed in Scotland, including their belief in superstition. "Part of each field was left barren as a sacrifice for him," Alita's mother continues. "It was in such a place my great-grandmother came across this Demon in disguise. It is true what Alita said. Our ancestor was thought to have more fire in her loins than brains in her head. But even she would not lay with the devil, no matter how charming he proved to be. He teased and cajoled and even tried to trick her. She would have none of it. She was a puzzle to Black Donald. A woman who could be so free with her wiles would not succumb to his. She did, however, agree to meet with him again. And again. Eventually, as she continued to thwart his attempts at seduction, a reluctant respect for her developed within him. Each time they met, their unlikely friendship grew. Finally, he came to care for her so much, he trusted her with his most precious secret. The secret to his demise." Doubtful expressions circulated the room like fireflies attempting to light the darkness.

Alita's mother ignored us and continued her story. "When my great-grandmother kept his secret, not telling a soul of what they spoke, Black Donald's trust grew even more. Finally, he had found a Cowan in which he could trust not only his most precious secret, but his most precious possession, as well. His blood."

At this point, I want to ask questions so badly my lips hurt. That is probably because they are currently mashed between my teeth as I struggle to keep them closed. Trickles of sound gurgle up my throat, the evidence of my unasked questions, but I stay strong and let her continue uninterrupted even though my lips will likely be permanently disfigured. The price I pay for speedy knowledge, I guess. Out of the corner of my eye, I see Kallen trying hard not to snicker at my struggle to remain silent. I am now struggling not to use my magic to pull his stool out from under him.

"Black Donald told my great-grandmother she would be the protector of Cowans, for he feared that one day his Demons would rise against him. If that happened, the Cowans would pay the price. Even though he was not particularly fond of Cowans in general, he did not like the idea that he was being plotted against. He wanted to spoil their plans if they succeeded in destroying him. He would not let them win all."

Okay, I lied. Her story does get interrupted. I really can't help myself. Turning to Isla, I blurt out, "You said the Demons were destroyed long before the Fairies came into existence. But, her story," I point at Alita's mother rather rudely, "implies that they were still around just a few centuries ago."

It is Kallen who responds to me. "Unless it was not a Demon who came to her great-grandmother."

I whirl around to question his idiocy. Then his meaning hits me. "I do believe she may have a brainwave or two that's still active," Taz drawls from my ankle. I kick at him but like usual, he's too fast for my foot to actually make contact.

Pretending my interruption didn't occur, Alita's mother continues once again. "He told her that only Cowans of her bloodline who bore goodness in their souls could carry this most sacred weapon. If their hearts soured, if their actions became even remotely like that of the Demons they may one day fight against, the weapon they carried within them would be destroyed. Then, there would be no one left who could fight the Demons when they came." Hence the fact that Alita thought this was a story her mother told her to make sure she was a good little girl.

After a moment of silence, it becomes apparent that Alita's mother has finished her story. I give it another few seconds just to make sure before I turn to Kallen and demand, "You think it was Raziel pretending to be Black Donald?"

Kallen shrugs. "If not Raziel, another Angel, yes."

"But why Alita's family?" Kegan asks, still not convinced any of this is real.

"Hook him up to an EEG machine and there'd be more than a few blips to account for," Taz snickers.

Unfortunately, he's too far away now to even try to kick him.

Kallen attempts to cue his cousin in. "Because Raziel knew the path her family line would take."

As each word sinks in, Kegan's face becomes harder and redder until he looks like a petrified apple. Not a scared apple, a hard as stone one. It's not a good look for him. "The bastard," he growls.

"How, exactly, did your great-grandmother receive the gift of this blood?" Isla asks delicately. Oh, good question. It's not like sleeping with an Angel would infuse Demon blood into her. Eew. Please tell me that Raziel did not sleep with Alita's great-grandmother.

"With magic," Alita's mother says simply.

A sigh of relief is expelled from my lips, which earns me some strange looks from around the room. "What, like I'm the only one relieved Raziel didn't sleep with her? Geesh." Kallen quirks an eyebrow at me as if to ask why it matters to me who Raziel slept with in the past. I quirk an eyebrow back saying he's my friend and it would gross me out if he slept with another friend's great-great-grandmother so stop being such a jealous bore. His eyes narrow, saying he's not being a jealous bore. I roll my eyes at this blatant denial of his so obvious actions.

He looks away, refusing to discuss this anymore. What a great thing about marriage. You get to know each other so well you can have entire conversations with your eyes and eyebrows.

"So, Raziel, or some other Angel, magically infused Demon blood with this Cowan woman's? This is far-fetched at best," Kegan insists.

"The proof is right here," Garren says, pointing at the prophecy. He is quite proud of himself for being one of the first to figure out what was going on.

Kegan's eyes follow his finger and he reads the prophecy for the first time. As he ingests the words, he begins to look less like a petrified red apple and more like a rotting green one. I'm fairly certain that's bile creeping up his throat which he needs to keep swallowing back down. Yuck. "My son is meant to be a weapon to fight Demons." This is not a question. He seems to have accepted this as fact now.

I shake my head adamantly. "Not happening. There is no way I am using Keelan as any type of weapon. It's ridiculous to even say it out loud," I declare. Yet, somewhere in the darkest recesses of my soul, I hear my fate laughing at me. Whenever I say never, the universe conspires to make me rue the word.

25 CHAPTER

"If it is his destiny, it cannot be denied any more than yours could." The look of utter defeat on Kegan's face as he says these words is hard to take in. I already feel morally desolate and I've blatantly refused to use his son as a weapon.

Placing my hands on my hips, I demand, "When have I ever simply given in to destiny without putting my own twist on it?"

This startles Kegan out of his too easily won self-defeat. "What?"

"She is correct, cousin. Xandra never does exactly as destiny bids her to do," Kallen says with a prideful grin in my direction. I do believe this is one of the things he loves about me. Good thing, because I'm not changing and he's stuck with me for eternity.

"Then what is it you plan to do?" Dagda asks impatiently with a pointed glance toward the back door. He would like his wife back sooner as opposed to later. I'm surprised he's been patient this long. I would have expected him to be ranting and raving and already insisting I hurry the hell up with whatever plan I have brewing. Not that I have a plan. And upon closer inspection, he is about two seconds away from telling me to hurry the hell up.

"I got nothing," I admit more to myself than anyone else in the room.

"I wonder if your grandfather had not run your mother off if I would have been able to do anything about your poor grammar?" an amused voice asks.

I whirl around to find my maternal grandmother standing there with open arms waiting for her hug. I don't hesitate like I would have when she was human. Technically, a Fallen Angel but no one knew that until the very end. Certainly not my grandfather. "Grandma!" I say as she hugs me tight. "Did you come to tell me what to do?"

Even snorts are pretty when they come from an Angel. "You know better than that, dear."

Disappointed like I usually am when I ask Angels for help, I back out of her embrace and mutter, "Then this is an odd time for a visit."

The Angel of Love reaches out and tucks a stray strand of my black hair behind my ear. "It is always a good time to visit my favorite granddaughter."

"I'm your only granddaughter," I point out. After a heartbeat, I add, "Aren't I?"

Grandma's laugh is a tinkle of pleasant sounds. "Of course you are, dear." Glancing toward the door, her eyes harden. They only soften slightly when she turns back to me. "You need to send those beasts back to the hell from which they sprang."

"Yeah, figured that one out on my own," I snark. I have come to love my grandmother, but she is still an Angel. And Angels can be really annoying.

"How did the Angels destroy them?" I ask. That's history, right? Surely she can explain history to me.

"We did not. We simply dwindled their numbers while unfortunately doing the same of our own."

That's encouraging. "Why have they taken so long to reappear?"

Grandma sighs. "Our war weakened them. We were never able to take out The Seven, but their dwindled numbers weakened them to the point they had to lay low. It is only the beacon which brings them to light now."

You can definitely tell Grandma recently spent time in the Cowan realm. What other Angel uses terms like 'take them out' and 'lay low'? "If they are so weak, why won't the Angels come and fight them now that they are out of hiding?"

Grandma's smile is tightlipped. I am definitely not going to like what she has to say. "We cannot."

"Why not?"

"There are many reasons."

Like I would ever accept an answer like that. Does she not know me at all? "Name a few," I push.

I get an exasperated sigh for my trouble. "Xandra, you know I cannot."

Beyond irritated, I throw my hands up in the air. "Do you guys sit in Angel time and take bets on who can frustrate me the most?"

This time, Grandma's sigh is sad. "Xandra, if I could take your burdens from you, I would gladly do so."

I hang my head which is now stuffed with guilt, and my neck is having a hard time with the strain. "I know you would. I'm just frustrated. What can you tell me?"

"Nothing, really. I simply wanted to encourage you. Just because the Angels and Demons reached a stalemate does not mean The Seven are indestructible. There are so many ingredients that go into winning a war, how is an innocent supposed to know such things or even have a specific agenda? Why, not that long ago, you would not have been able to discern between good and evil, much less put up detectable defenses against your enemies, even unconscious ones. Now, you are so confused about your Angel heritage and your occasional wings with a few tarnished feathers and your Witch and Fairy and Cowan blood all mixed together, how in the world would you know the recipe? You have so many other things to worry about right now, such as saving your true blooded Angel friends and their wings, I really just wanted to check in and see what you were making of things. Your magic is so strong, but only the most gullible believe themselves infallible to all charms and spells." Without even pausing for a breath, my grandmother pulls me into her arms and finishes with, "Take care my precious dear, for I expect you to live long enough to give me great-grandchildren who can stand up proud and strong as they follow the light of their own grandchildren when the time comes. Remember, I am always here for you in your time of need, just as all the Angels are, even if we need to be the silent supporters in the background and let you do the actual fighting."

I do not even have a chance to part my lips to explain to her that this was by far the worst pep talk I have ever received before Grandma pops me back out of Angel time. Yup, she's my grandmother, but damn is she annoying sometimes.

26 CHAPTER

"I got nothing?" Dagda roars as I reenter the Fairy realm of existence.

Since I have been conversing with my grandmother for the last several minutes, it takes me a moment to backtrack and figure out what he's talking about. Oh, yeah. The last thing he heard me say was, 'I got nothing.' Surprisingly, he doesn't comment on my atrocious grammar like Grandma did. Things are pretty grim when my biological father forgets to be the grammar police.

I open my mouth to tell them I've been talking to Grandma, when I snap my lips closed. Why should I bother? It's not like she said anything to help us and it will just frustrate them as much as it does me that the Angels refuse to get involved. Even when the Demons are technically their oldest enemy. I notice Kallen giving me an odd look, though. He already suspects my conversation with an Angel even if he doesn't know which one. He's gotten really good at detecting when I'm pulled into Angel time. He doesn't say anything, though. He figures if I learned anything useful, I'd share with the group.

A painful tug on my magic has me yelping. Several others in the room also grimace in pain. This is not good. "Stay here!" I shout to no one in particular as I rush to the door. Several Fairies do follow me, but only the ones whose magic is also being affected.

Outside, I skid to a halt. I thought seeing one Demon was disturbing. Seeing six of them at once is enough to sear my retinas with ugly. They are horrible, offensive looking creatures. It turns out the first one I saw was a real looker compared to the rest. These guys are just nasty. They have the same charred skin the first one had, but theirs is torn and tattered, exposing pieces of the inner Demon. This consists of muscles which seem to be riddled with gangrene and maggots. Blood and pus ooze from various cuts and orifices. One has an eye which is resting more on its cheek bone than in its actual eye socket. It looks like they have just come from battle, but their wounds are far from fresh looking. I'm going to go out on a limb here and say that when Demons are injured, they don't heal. They keep living, but they don't heal. Meaning, these wounds are from eons of battles fought. Wow. And they want to keep living? I'm sorry, if my insides were mostly comprised of gangrene and maggots, I might have to question what there really is to live for at that point.

The disgusting Demons are not paying attention to us. They are paying attention to their friend in the magical cage. Chanting in the same ancient language the Demon who possessed Tana had, they are trying to free him. From the painful ripping and tearing of our magic, I would say they are fairly close to succeeding.

"Are they chanting the de-possession spell?" Dagda asks. I have never seen him so consumed with panic.

Because of this, I hate to be the bearer of bad tidings, but I must. "I don't think so, no." He gets my meaning. They are planning to take Tana with them. I throw even more magic at the cage, as do the others, but the Demons keep right on chanting.

I would try to fight the Demons, take them on one by one or as a group, but I don't dare deflect any of my magic. Right now, the important thing is to protect Tana. A small pinch on my back tells me my Angel wings have appeared and I shout, "Close your eyes!" Concentrating hard, I throw everything I have into it. A blinding white light emanates from me and my wings and blasts forward. Several of the Demons roar in pain. Suddenly, they take notice of us. Their chanting stops and they focus all of their attention and magic on us.

"Keep your magic on the cage!" Kallen shouts. I don't believe he's talking to me. I felt Isla and Dagda start to pull back in order to fight the Demons, too. No, that can't happen. They need to protect Tana while I focus on the Demons.

Unfortunately, six Demons is a lot to handle. Our magic meets and the air bursts into flames around the point of impact. Oxygen is quite combustible, after all. The explosion rocks the house. Around me, a couple of Fairies, the ones closest to the blast, and several Demons drop to the ground. I barely remain standing.

It's enough. The loss of a couple of key players whose magic was holding the cage together is enough to let it come crumbling down under the force of the Demons still standing. It takes but a second for them to grab Tana and disappear.

All six of them are gone. Several were wounded, but they apparently had enough strength still to teleport. Damn it! At least they left with a few more wounds which will never, ever heal.

Glancing around me, I am suddenly much less satisfied by this knowledge. Garren is burned almost beyond recognition. Isla, who was close to him, suffers from several serious burns but this fact is lost on her as she gathers her husband into her arms. She is crying. Isla is crying. Not gentle weeping, but gut wrenching sobs of grief. No, he can't be dead.

I scramble toward them. As I pass Dagda, I see the utter destruction of his soul in his eyes. The guilt of not being able to save his wife. The bitterness toward me that I couldn't, either. I know in my heart that the bitterness will pass, he won't hold me responsible for what the Demons did. But, in this moment, his heart can do nothing else. After all, I am supposed to be the one who saves everyone from evil, right?

"Xandra!" Isla croaks through her sobs. "Help him. Please!"

Only when I hear her voice do I realize I stopped. It was not seeing Dagda's expression, or Isla's grief, or even Garren looking more Demon than Fairy because of his burns that shocked me into stopping. No. It is the fact that I have a perfectly white Angel feather in my pocket. And it's not mine.

27 CHAPTER

My feet are moving once more and in a second, I am dropping to my knees next to Isla and Garren. I have my hands on the latter's still sizzling skin in a heartbeat and I am pulling magic again. I try to be as gentle as I can, but time is of the essence. I can feel Garren's life force trying to slip away.

So can Isla. "You stay with me, damn it!" she growls into her husband's ear. "You were stubborn enough to wait for me all those years, you better be stubborn enough to stay with me now. I will never, ever forgive you if you do not. Not this time," she growls. In a quieter, for his ears only, voice, she adds, "I love you so much. I cannot lose you."

I don't know how long it takes to heal him. Slowly, exposed tissue under Garren's burned skin begins to mend. Not long after, the skin itself knits itself into whole tissue once again. After what seems like forever, a small cough emanates from his chest. A second later, a louder cough and a gasp as he draws a large breath into his bruised lungs. Garren's eyes fly open and lock onto Isla's face. The relief at seeing her alive and well is so dramatic, I fear he would slip into shock again if I wasn't still in the process of healing him. Isla hugs him tighter. Since she is touching him, my healing magic has been slipping into her, as well. Her own wounds are fading quickly.

When Garren is once again whole, I turn to Dagda. He was also injured in the blast. His right leg is bleeding and possibly broken. It takes me a minute to figure out how that happened. Then, I notice that chunks of the house were ripped off with the blast. He was hit by debris. I move toward him, prepared to heal him next.

Holding up a hand, Dagda growls. "I am fine. Focus your energy on finding my wife."

I shake my head. "I need your help if I'm going to do that. We have a lot of work to do, and you being injured will make you useless."

"Work," he scoffs. "We have no idea what work we need to do to bring her back."

"Speak for yourself," I mutter, moving within touching range. Despite his grumbling, when I kneel down next to him, he lets me heal his leg. I don't get a chance to check him for other injuries. As soon as he can walk, he is on his feet and striding toward the house.

Kallen comes to me and offers his hand to help me up. "He is angrier with himself than anyone else," he says softly.

I nod. "I know. I still can't believe we lost her to them, though."

His lips pressed into a grim line, Kallen agrees. "Neither can I." Wrapping his arms around me, he says with all the faith in the universe, "We will get her back."

I smile up at my adoring and sexy husband. "We will, and I know how."

He studies my face trying to determine if I am being optimistic, or if I truly have a plan. "Do tell," he says.

I shake my head. "I don't think I should say the plan out loud." I glance around. "Who knows who could be listening." After all, the others were watching us on Demon television earlier. The Demons could be watching us all the time.

Kallen nods in understanding. "Very well." He turns to his grandmother and Garren who are rising from the driveway. Garren is still a little weak so he is leaning on Isla as they begin to walk to the house. "Let me help you," Kallen calls.

His arms drop from me and he hurries to help his step-grandfather into the house. I follow the three of them in. Clutching the feather in my pocket, I begin to make a mental list of the things I will need to bring about the destruction of the Demons. They are going to regret ever coming up against me and my family.

28 CHAPTER

As I enter the house, Grandma's little pep talk plays through my mind again. I thought it strange at the time that someone who helped orchestrate my birth would forget which blood lines I had running through my veins. My grandfather is a Witch from a long line of Witches. She is an Angel. My biological father is a Fairy. There is not a drop of Cowan blood in my veins. But, apparently, the recipe she gave me calls for Cowan blood. I guess her little speech turned out to be one hell of a pep talk after all. Unfortunately, I can't say this out loud. No one else even knows I spoke to her.

Before anyone can say anything, I hold a hand up. "I need a few minutes to think, please."

"Is there anything we should be doing while you are thinking?" Kallen asks pointedly. He is the only one who knows I already have a plan formulating.

"We do not have time for this, we need to do something," Dagda growls.

I turn and give him a pointed look. "I know," I growl right back.

Kallen steps in. "Uncle, perhaps we should continue researching. You know Xandra works best when left to her own devices." He also gives the Fairy a pointed look.

Dagda is really freaking dense today. I blame it on the fact that his possessed wife was just kidnapped by Demons. I imagine all of his brain power is leached onto that fact and that fact alone. "I am not going to sit here reading books! We will travel to the hell dimension and rescue Tana!" He stalks toward me. "You will teleport us there."

Placing my hands on my hips, I stand my ground as he approaches. "Listen, I need a minute and you are going to give me one. Even if that means I put you in a magical cage."

"Dagda," Isla says sharply and his head whips in her direction. It's a good thing she's not a delicate flower, otherwise she would wilt under the evil glare he is shooting her way. "Trust her." That's all she says. Trust her.

I turn my own shocked eyes in her direction. She knows I'm up to something. Hmm. Am I that transparent? I really hope not. Otherwise, we'll have a Demon infestation problem before I'm ready for them.

Dagda opens his mouth to say something when Kallen and Kegan move as one. They each grab an arm and forcefully push him down onto a stool. He is so shocked he doesn't even lash out with magic or fists. "What the hell do you think you are doing?" he demands.

"Saving you from yourself. And saving Tana," Kallen says evenly. "If we could save her with brute force, we would have done so outside. Now, we need a plan. A plan your daughter will make as soon as you leave her be." There is so much steel in his voice, I expect a fully formed skyscraper to spring from his mouth.

It works. Dagda is still pissed and impatient, but he doesn't say another word to me. He doesn't pick up a book, either, but that's okay. I doubt there's anything in any of these books that would be particularly useful anyway.

Still, the Demons don't know that I know that. I turn to everyone else. "You should keep reading," I tell them.

Reluctantly, several books are opened and perused. They all seem to know it's a waste of time, but they are keeping up appearances to give me time. Wow, my family knows me well.

Okay, now that I don't have a crazed father breathing down my neck, I can focus once again on Grandma's speech. First, though, I marvel at how skillfully she came to me and presented me with the information I need. Did she do it on her own, or was she given permission? I really hope it's the latter. I don't want Grandma to lose her wings over this.

I begin my mental checklist. I need a tarnished feather from my own set of wings. Fortunately, I still have them on my back. I reach over and grab one of the feathers that turned black because of a previous action on my part. "Stupid black feathers," I complain and yank it out. "Ow! If I had known it was going to hurt that much, I would have left it there." That was for the benefit of any watching Demons. It did hurt a surprising amount, though. I really hope another one grows in its place. Not that you can tell I'm missing a feather, but it still seems wrong to tear out an Angel feather.

Which reminds me of the feather in my pocket. I'm going to leave it there for now. Grandma must have slipped me one of her feathers when she gave me a hug. The feather of a full blooded Angel, another ingredient on her list. She didn't come out and say that I needed the feather, but her speech about my true blooded friends and their wings and the fact she slipped it in my pocket is enough for me to figure this out all on my own. I'm smart that way.

Now for the blood. I need the blood of a Cowan. I apparently also need the blood of a Witch, a Fairy and an Angel. Those I can supply myself. Lucky for me, a Cowan happened to walk into the room not that long ago. I could go upstairs and get the blood from Dad, or even Zac, but I don't want to raise any more suspicion than necessary. But, how to go about it? I can't ask for it. I guess I get creative.

Hmm, creative bloodletting. I could juggle knives and claim it helps me think better. Nope. Much more likely to hurt myself than others in that scenario. I could trip and knock Alita's mother off her stool and hope she bleeds somewhere before healing her. No, too risky that she might not bleed and then she'd be spooked and avoid being near me. I could simply ask everyone for a blood sample 'just in case'. Then they would ask 'just in case what' and I'm really bad at coming up with excuses for my stupid behavior.

"You okay over there? You look like you're considering a bowel movement. Or is that really your thinking face?" Taz snarks.

I glower in his direction when a thought hits me. "What's the matter, been too long without bacon? How about I have someone find you a piece?" I ask in a deceptively sympathetic tone.

Taz is instantly suspicious. "You never offer me food."

"It's a new world," I say with a saccharine smile. Turning to Alita's mother, I ask, "Would you mind looking in the fridge? Tabitha keeps some bacon strips for when Taz is feeling faint from weight loss if he hasn't eaten in an hour or so."

Tabitha glares at me. "I do not overfeed your mongrel." Moving from her spot, she says with a sniff, "But I will get him a snack since you knocked him unconscious earlier. He probably needs the sustenance."

I refrain from snorting. Taz could go weeks living on his fat stores before he needed sustenance. "No, I need you to be doing research. Alita's mom should get it." Tabitha gives me a funny look, but she stops walking.

Alita's mom glances back and forth between us. "Should I get the bacon?"

"Yes, please," I say with a polite smile. Then, I turn to Taz. "No biting," I warn. "You know how to take things gently from someone's hand."

To my great surprise, Taz doesn't argue. He just stares at me a minute, trying to figure out what my game is. I know he's figured it out when he grumbles, "Bite one lousy person and you never live it down." In truth, he's only bitten bad guys. Never someone who is feeding him. He would never, ever risk that person not feeding him again.

Alita's mother finds the bacon and walks uncertainly toward Taz. She stops several feet away and looks back at me. "Does he really bite?" she asks.

I wave a hand like it's a stupid question. "Of course not," I assure her.

Tabitha is actually offended for Taz. "He is gentle as a lamb when it comes to food," she insists, glaring at me for giving the impression otherwise.

Alita's mother moves closer to my Familiar and dangles the bacon over him. After a minute, she realizes he's not a dog and isn't going to jump for it. She opens her fingers to drop it in front of him. Realizing it's now or never, Taz lunges. I have never seen him get so much air in a leap without attacking a bad guy. Then again, that's the only time he leaps, or exercises in general. Which makes this leap so impressive for such a fat little thing. Wow. Before the bacon slice even leaves her fingers, he has latched onto it. And her index finger. Ouch. Taz and I are definitely going to have to make that up to her. There is blood spurting from her finger. I think he may have cut through an artery with one of his incisors. Blood is going everywhere. I will have plenty of blood to choose from.

There are gasps around the room. "Has the thing gone rabid?" Dagda demands.

On the floor, Taz spits the bacon out of his mouth. "I can't believe she got her blood on my bacon," he moans. "I can't eat that." Next to him, Felix snickers.

"Oh no!" I cry in mock alarm. "Let me heal that for you." I rush to Alita's mother's side and grab her hand. I still have the feather I pulled from my wing in my hand and it just happens to get soaked with blood. Oops. Before the woman bleeds out on the kitchen floor, though, I hurry up and heal her. As I'm doing this, I try hard to ignore the glare I am getting from her daughter. Alita may know I am up to something, but she is not pleased this something involved me instructing my Familiar to viciously attack her mother.

As for Taz, he is trying really hard to get the woman's blood off his tongue. He has now resorted to licking the floor to wipe it off. Considering the fact that Tasmanian devils are the trash can of the forest and will eat dead carcasses, this seems strange to me. "Being a little dramatic, aren't you?" I ask out of the side of my mouth.

"Have you ever tasted blood tainted with Demon blood?" he snaps, now wiping his tongue with the bottom of his dirty paw.

"Nope," I say probably more cheerily than necessary. The reply I get is too rude to repeat.

"Will you please get on with your *thinking*?" Dagda snarls.

"So sorry I had to keep Alita's mom from bleeding out," I grumble.

"It was not such a dire wound," the woman points out. But, she has moved to the other side of the room, as far from Taz as possible.

Okay, I have the feathers and the Cowan blood. Now, I need my own blood. I glance around the kitchen trying to devise an accident of my own. Though, at this point, I could probably convince Taz to bite me. He's pretty pissed about the Demon blood thing. How was I supposed to know it would leave such a bad taste in his mouth? I am far from being a Demonologist.

Moving to my side, Kallen asks softly, "Is there anything I can help with as you ponder the weight of the universe?"

Can he? I do get the feeling I am running out of time. The Demons will probably attack again soon, so I should speed things along. I consider the plan forming in my mind. After a moment, I smile up at him. "In about thirty seconds, you can hold your cousin back."

"What?!" Kegan's head swings back and forth between Kallen and me. "What do you mean, hold me back?"

Instead of answering him, I teleport across the room. Laying my hand on Alita's mother's arm, I teleport to her daughter. Alita is holding Keelan in her arms and her eyes open wide in alarm when we are suddenly by her side. I don't give her a chance to react other than that. I reach out and touch her and teleport the four of us away. The last thing I hear is Kegan's anguished cry as he watches his family disappear.

I block the sound out and focus on what I am doing. Usually when I teleport, I have a specific destination in mind. This time, I have no idea where I am going. As the magic takes hold, I concentrate on Keelan instead. He is the map. He will lead us where we need to go and I push my magic toward him, using sheer force of will to make him our guide. I just hope my dear friends will forgive me for what I am about to do with their son.

29 Chapter

I expected hell to be hot. After all, the Demons walk around with charred flesh all the time. Of course it's going to be hot. I did not expect it to be so hot my own flesh would begin to sear. I turn frightened eyes to my kidnapping victims, fearing I have already put Keelan in too much danger. To my utter surprise, the trio has hardly broken a sweat. Must be the Demon blood flowing through their veins making them less susceptible. After all, it's probably taken millennia for the Demons to look as bad as they do.

We are in a dark tunnel. At least, I think it's a tunnel. I reach my arms out and I feel walls on either side. Then a frightening thought hits me. What if we are in a box? I frantically throw my arms in different directions and am greatly relieved when I do not find more walls.

"Xandra, what have you done?" Alita asks, a mixture of fear, disappointment and 'I am going to rip you apart with my bare hands if anything happens to my son' in her voice. And I was worried giving birth would send her back to being shy, timid Alita. If anything, it has made her fiercer. That's good. She's going to need that strength.

"Made a bloody mess of things, it seems," a voice says from my ankle. Taz and Felix latched onto me before we left. I'm still trying to figure out how they did it. I wasn't planning to bring them. But, they were waiting for me when I teleported to Alita's side and I couldn't shake them before I teleported away. They are fast and strong little suckers when they want to be.

Before I can open my mouth to respond, the tunnel begins to light up. It is not a bright light. More of a dull, bluish light. But, it's enough for us to see by. Which is why I am able to see Alita almost drop her son. Both her mother and I reach out, placing our arms under hers in case she loses her grip altogether.

"What is happening to him?" Alita demands.

"He is showing us the way," I say simply. "He's the dark beacon."

"Otherwise known as a freak of nature," Taz mutters. I ignore him per usual.

Felix does not. "Shut it," he growls. I expect Taz to argue, but I think being in a Demon tunnel in hell has taken some of the fight out of him. Or, he's simply conserving his energy. I really hope it's option number two.

"Beacons lead Fairies to them, not the other way around," Alita points out.

I wave her off. "Semantics." Sobering, I add, "It is his destiny to bring Demons into the light, even if he has to bring the light to them."

"Xandra, I don't know what you are up to, but send my mother home. Now," Alita demands in a voice that brooks no argument.

Unfortunately, I need to argue. "I can't. She is as necessary a part of this as Keelan is."

I can just make out Alita's eyes narrowing in the dark tunnel. "So, you will use my son after all."

Guilt washes over me. I want to tell her to trust me, that things will be fine. If only I could say the words in a way that would sound like I meant them. Right now, I am taking the biggest gamble of my life. Of all of our lives. So, the only word I say is, "Yes."

"I will never forgive you if any harm comes to him."

"I know," I nod. I won't forgive myself. I assume she can see that in my eyes until I remember how dark it is in here. I open my mouth to say the words aloud, but again, I remember where I am. Who knows who could be listening. So, instead, I say, "This is the only way to save everyone."

Before she can argue more, I reach out and take Keelan from her. It happens so fast and I take her so unaware, Alita isn't able to stop me. She does reach out to try to take him back, but she is rebuffed by the wall of magic I put up around myself and the baby. From the betrayal and devastation sitting in my friend's eyes, I know in my heart that may be a term I will not be able to describe her with in the future. Moral desolation, I have arrived.

I begin walking and the others follow. Taz and Felix are outside of my magic but they are close on my heals. If there wasn't a magical barrier between us, I would be tripping over them they are so close to me. I take two steps in one direction before I notice the light emanating from Keelan dims. I turn and walk the other way. The more steps I take, the brighter he glows. Not him, exactly. It is more like he has an aura around him. A blue, glowing aura.

There are several twists and turns in the tunnel, and several times we are given the choice of taking different routes. It doesn't take me long to figure out this is not simply a tunnel, but a labyrinth. If we didn't have Keelan here to guide us, we would have been lost at the first choice of tunnels. I have a terrible sense of direction and get turned around easily. Plus, I have no idea where we are trying to go.

Behind me, Alita and her mother are walking hand in hand. I kind of expected tears and panic from her mom. After all, she is a Cowan and doesn't possess even a hint of magic and she is in a Demon lair. But, she is walking with clear eyes and a sense of purpose. She will fight to the last to protect her daughter and grandchild if need be. I personally hope it doesn't come to that, but I applaud her courage.

After a century or two, we finally see something ahead of us other than dark tunnel walls. It's not a light at the end of the tunnel. No, I don't think this place has anything that resembles true light. At least not of the solar kind. It is a flickering light. Probably from a fire. Hopefully not a giant fire pit like the hell from religions back home is described as. I would really prefer not to fall into a giant fire pit at the moment. I'm already sweating so much my skin is peeling under the moisture. Tabitha can whip up a great deodorant with her herbs and magic, but it definitely does not stand up to the heat of Demon hell. If I make it home, I seriously doubt Kallen will want me rushing into his arms until after I've had a shower.

We reach the end of the tunnel and Felix lets out a low whistle. At least, the closest sound to a whistle a creature with no lips can make. It's actually more of a high pitched hum/exhale kind of thing. "Not much of a life for the other thirteen, is it?"

No, it isn't. We have come to a large cavern, and by large, I mean colosseum large. The floor of the cavern is several stories down from us. With no way to get there other than to teleport, which I am not quite willing to do yet.

This is not an opulent cavern like the ones Hades has in hell. There are no buffet tables or comfy chairs. There is no furniture at all. The only thing in the cavern other than thirteen Demons is a blazing fire which is shooting flames a good twenty to thirty feet in the air. With each burst of light and heat, the layers of my skin deteriorate even more. At least I'm not sweating anymore. The air is so hot here, any moisture coming from my skin has instantly evaporated. Unfortunately, my eye sockets are trying to do the same thing. I glance down at my Familiars and find they are blinking maniacally like I am in an effort to generate lubrication. Alita, her mother and Keelan do not have this same issue. They are hot and uncomfortable, but not on the verge of passing out like I am.

The Demons, oddly enough, are also on the verge of passing out. I suspect this is because they have been exposed to this inferno for millennia. No living creature could be surrounded by this much heat and not succumb to it eventually. It just probably took them longer than most. But it has taken its toll. They are not moving. One may flick a hand or twitch its head every now or then, but for the most part, they are lying where they fell to the ground at some point. I seriously doubt there is any propagating going on anymore. These Demons can hardly move. Which explains why they have not replenished their numbers over the years following their war with the Angels.

Is this lethargy also a side effect of having all of their power syphoned away to be used by The Seven? No wonder they never revolted. I don't remember who said the rest of the Demon population didn't mind the sacrifice for The Seven, but I think they were misinformed. It's not that these Demons don't mind, it's that they are unable to resist.

"Do you believe it is safe to go down there?" Felix asks.

I cock a brow at him. "Safe? I don't think it's safe to go anywhere near Demons wherever you are."

A snort comes from behind me. "Yet you brought my son here."

Guilt washes through me but I tamp it down. This is the only way, I repeat over and over in my head. When that doesn't work, I make the decision to push on. "We need to find The Seven," I announce.

"Do you see a door anywhere down there? If so, you are having hallucinations," Taz informs me.

"There must be a way out," I argue.

"There," Alita points. I follow her finger and can just make out what she is pointing at.

Squinting, I ask, "Is that another tunnel entrance?" If so, it is just as high up as this one. Someone does not want those Demons down there to have any chance of escape.

Reading my mind, Taz muses, "I guess the masses don't get to leave that room. Ever." After a heartbeat, he adds, "I wonder why it's not littered with excrement."

I scowl down at him. "Does it really matter what Demons do with their poop?"

He shrugs his little shoulders. "I possess great curiosity. Something your feeble brain can obviously not appreciate."

"I would assume they simply throw it in the fire," Felix points out reasonably. I cannot believe he joined the conversation.

"You are probably right," Taz agrees.

Shaking my head, I snap, "We're going to the next tunnel. Maybe on the way out we stop in below and you can figure out where Demons do their business."

"Much appreciated," Taz says with a nod of his head like he thinks I'm being serious. I just roll my eyes.

Turning to Alita and her mother, I say, "I am going to let my magic go. Are you going to fight me on going forward?"

Alita cocks her head to the side. "Would it do any good?"

I shake my head and respond honestly. "No."

"Why will you not tell us what is going on? Why did you bring us here?" Alita's eyes slip to her mother. "I mean, I know why you brought Keelan, and I assume you brought me because he's my son. But, why did you bring my mother?"

With a heavy sigh, I say pointedly, "You know, I wish I could tell you. Chances are we are being observed, though…"

Fear radiates through both Alita and her mother and they both glance around nervously. After a second, Alita squares her shoulders and brings her eyes back to mine. "I am going to trust you. For now. But, I want to hold my son."

Thank god. Who knew babies could get so heavy? Letting my magic go, I gladly return Keelan to the arms of his mother. For the briefest of seconds, I see the idea of fleeing pass through Alita's eyes. It must dawn on her that she just exited a labyrinth to which she has no map and she decides against it.

Reaching out, I grab hold of both Alita and her mother's arms. Felix and Taz grab on to me. None too gently I might add. I am definitely going to talk to them about just how deeply they need to sink their teeth into my flesh to come along with me. Definitely not this deep.

Reading my mind once again, Taz says, "Um, Xandra, that's not us biting you."

Did he read my mind or did I speak my thoughts out loud? That thought is immediately pushed out of my head by the next one. "What?!" My eyes shoot to my ankle and sure enough, something is biting me, but it's not one of my Familiars. Felix extends his snout and rips the Demon rat away. Along with some of my flesh. Immediately, I begin to feel woozy. Not from blood loss.

I'm pretty sure the nasty little rat just poisoned me. It was probably following us waiting for me to release my magic so it could bite me. I knew this was all too easy until now.

30 Chapter

Poison or no, we need to make it to the other tunnel. "Hold on tight," I tell everyone. Pulling magic, sluggish, heavy magic, I imagine us on the other side of the cavern in a hole in the wall just like the one we're standing in. I am ever so relieved when I open my eyes and find us there.

"Xandra, are you alright?" Alita's mother asks. She is probably asking because I just fell to my knees. Always the first clue someone is not alright and is probably about to pass out.

No, I refuse to pass out. I have a plan, damn it. I will not let the Demons win. The Angels, Grandma specifically, gave me the recipe. I mixed it together. Hopefully I measured everything correctly. It's not like they told me if I would need a thimbleful of blood or a whole bucket of it.

Blood. That reminds me. I haven't mixed it all together. I have a feather doused with Cowan blood, but I haven't added mine to it yet. I need to rectify that. Holding my hand out, I mumble, "Bite me."

"Screw you, too," Taz snarks back.

I shake my head and the walls of the tunnel waver. "No, I mean actually bite me."

"Xandra," Felix says in such a calm, soothing voice I want to lie down next to him and take a nap. That could be the poison, though. "There is no need for subterfuge now. Create a knife."

Create a knife? Why would I do that? Oh, because I don't need to trick myself into giving up my blood. I can just cut myself. I give Felix a lopsided grin. "Good plan." I do create a knife and I do cut myself. Not on the palm like they always do in TV shows and movies. Who the hell would cut their palm like that? That would hurt like a son of a bitch. Do they not know how many nerve endings are in a palm? Those directors need to take a few anatomy lessons. And it's not like the blood coming out of a palm is different than the blood coming out of say my wrist. No. Wrists are bad, too. Anyway, blood is blood. It doesn't matter where it comes from and it doesn't need to be something showy like a palm. Just below my elbow. Yes. That's a good place to take a little blood from. Just a little nick in my skin. Um, that might have been too deep. Actually, I didn't even realize I already had the knife in my hand. Wow. This poison is really messing with my head.

"She is going to pass out," a voice says from far away. It's a pleasant, motherly voice. Alita's mother. Yes, it's her voice.

I force my hand to move. It's starting to become painful to move. I think my joints are beginning to lock up. Still, I force my hand into my pocket and take out the feather from Grandma's wing. I use it to wipe the blood from my arm.

"You could have created a tissue, you know," Taz grumbles. But there's no force behind his words. He's afraid of what's happening to me and just trying to hide his feelings behind snark.

I finish mopping up the blood, all the while hoping the poison running through my veins isn't going to taint the spell. When it is thoroughly soaked, I pull out the other feather and I mash them together. I expect there to be a sizzling sound or something. I am sorely disappointed.

Waving a hand about toward no one in particular, I say, "Help me up."

"It is doubtful you can stand right now," Felix says unhelpfully.

"We need to keep going," I insist.

"Why don't you heal yourself first?" Taz asks. Is it my imagination or did he say that like I'm a complete idiot?

"I can't heal this," I slur. My tongue, I believe, has doubled in size. "It's attacking my Angel blood. This is how they killed Angels." I don't know how I know that. Some innate sense, maybe?

"You are dying?" Alita gasps.

I scrunch my face up in the best scowl I can manage while my nerves are refusing to communicate in full sentences to my muscles. "Not if I can help it."

Arms slide under my armpits and I am suddenly heaved to my feet. Wow, Alita's mom is really strong. Must be all that gardening she does. "Come along then. I will help you."

"Should we not turn back?" Alita asks. "We need to get you help."

I shake my head and instantly regret it. The pain from the poison is really starting to set in. Unless I actually do have a thousand tiny soldiers firing tanks in my skull.

Could happen in the world I live in. "We go forward," I slur.

As we start walking, well I'm hobbling and they are walking, Alita's mother says, "I wondered why the Demons were not coming after us."

"Sent rats to do their dirty work," I grumble. Ow, ow, ow. My legs hurt like hell now. I think the poison is made from the hell fire in the pit, because I believe it is literally burning through my veins and soft tissue.

My vision is dimming around the edges but I can still see the soft glow emanating from Keelan. Alita and he are taking the lead now. Taz is walking in front of me and Felix is following behind. Both are on the lookout for more rats. I doubt any more are coming. It seems one was enough to do me in.

After another century or two, we finally see something other than dark walls and other tunnels. Once again there is the flickering of light. Flames. Not a raging inferno like the last one. This one is smaller with significantly less heat emanating from it. Thank goodness. I don't know if I could deal with the pain from the poison and the moisture sucking flames of the cavern.

When Alita stops abruptly, her mother and I run into her. What do you know, my skin is just as sensitive as my insides. "Ow!" I exclaim louder than I should. Though, it's not like they don't already know we're here, or that I'm in pain. "Keep going," I urge through clenched teeth.

"I cannot," Alita says. "My feet will not move."

My eyebrows try really hard to furrow. "Literally?"

This earns me a sour look. "No. I am scared." For her son. I know Alita better than to think that she would not face Demons on her own if it meant saving everyone she loves.

"Me, too," I assure her.

"Liar."

She is right. I'm too painful to be scared. Pissed off and ready to get this over with is more like it. It is my sincerest hope that before I kill the damn Demons I can torture a recipe for an antitoxin out of them. Hopefully one exists. "We need to do this," I tell her.

"I know." Alita stares down at her son with the saddest expression I have ever seen in my life. "It is his destiny to die to save the universe."

I open my mouth to say something about that but clamp it shut when a figure moves at the end of the tunnel. So, instead I say, "We found them."

"Yes," a voice calls. It's Tana's voice. "You have."

Damn, I really hope this day doesn't end with me having to kill Tana. Whether I have good reason or not, Dagda would never forgive me.

31 Chapter

"We've come to make a trade," I call as loudly as my constricting vocal cords will allow. I urge Alita's mother to help me keep walking. We need to confront all seven of the Demons, and I seriously doubt they are going to crowd into the tunnel to accommodate us.

A snarl curls up Tana's lips. "You are dying. You are in no position to make a deal." She shows no signs of moving from the end of the tunnel as we approach. Is she supposed to keep us out?

"We both know that isn't true," I counter. I don't know that, I'm bluffing. We'll see how that goes. "There is the prophecy, after all."

Tana's face furrows into a frown. "You lower beings and your prophecies. Lies spoken by immortal tongues to scare the masses."

"Yeah, most of the them," I admit. "Except this one. It was written by an omniscient Angel. He said the birth of a dark beacon would bring you guys scurrying into the light and he was right."

There is a roar behind Tana that curdles my blood. I have never heard a cry of anger and frustration such as this. There should be a recording of it in an online dictionary, for it truly conveys the emotions like no words I've read or sound I've ever heard. Even if you had really bad speakers on your computer or laptop, you'd still get the gist of it.

"We need to keep going," I murmur to Alita and her mother under the noise of the continued scream. I have goosebumps over my entire body now from the sound. "We need to get into that room."

They oblige me. When we are just a few yards away, I take advantage of the fact that Demon infested Tana is distracted. She is partially turned away from us, trying to shush the Demon making all the racket. Summoning the last bit of strength I have, I send out a burst of magic. Tana goes flying. It is an oddly satisfying spectacle on many levels. Mostly, I am excited to get the better of the Demon inside her. It is caught completely off guard. And, because I am addled by poison, I will admit that a tiny part of me has regretted never being able to get the teensiest revenge against Tana for the things she did to me and my loved ones when she was evil. Yes, I've grown to care for her a great deal since then. But, still. If you can't be completely honest when you're dying of poison, when can you be?

This gives us enough time to push over the threshold. Gasps emit from Alita and her mother's mouths. I don't have the energy to gasp. I simply let my mouth gape open. It may have already been doing that from lack of muscle control, but it's the thought that counts.

Suddenly, we find ourselves in an alternate reality. The Demons may have been laying low over the last few millennia, but they certainly have been paying attention. The disgust I detected toward the Cowans earlier was a ruse, apparently. At least, they are not disgusted by Cowan possessions and tastes even if they despise the actual beings. For we have stepped inside what looks very much like a high rise apartment in someplace like New York. There are ultramodern furnishings and even a carpet on the floor. I half expect track lighting, but electricity is lacking in this part of the universe, I guess. Instead, there are fire places surrounding the walls filled with the same hell fire that roared in the cavern behind us. A muted version of it anyway.

It is strange seeing the Demons in such an environment. At least they didn't make the mistake of picking white furniture. Part of them is probably left behind when they jump to their feet and the black leather of their furniture probably disguises this fact. Unless their furniture was once white cloth and this has happened so many times that it only appears to be black leather now. That thought is so disgusting I don't even want to contemplate it any longer. So, I turn my attention to the annoyed Demons holding cocktail glasses full of some sort of dark liquor and glaring at me.

"You made it passth the pit," one lisps. He would have benefitted from the services of a speech pathologist when he was young.

"Yeah, I'm good like that," I snark.

Demon infused Tana lifts itself from the floor, red flushing across her face. It's probably embarrassed that it's weakened state of possession allowed it to be such an easy target for my magic. "She came to offer a trade. The child for this body." The Demon glares down at Tana's body and I can almost see the images dancing in its mind over what it wants to do with it. Permanently marring ranking probably only slightly above killing it slowly and painfully.

Alita rears on me. "You are going to trade Keelan for Tana?"

"Um…no. I was planning to trade Keelan for all the beings of the universe."

"I hate you."

"I know. But, it is too late to stop this now." Without the help of her mother, who is too disgusted to touch me now, I shuffle closer to Alita. I reach out and gently stroke Keelan's soft, downy cheek. I know his mother wants to snatch him out of my reach, but she doesn't. She allows me to adjust his little blanket with sad hands. "You will always be loved," I whisper. Forcing myself to meet Alita's hateful gaze, I add, "No one will ever love you as much as your mother."

Now, Alita does snatch him away. Holding him close to her heart, she growls, "I will never forgive you for this. Ever."

I nod. "I know that, too." Turning back to The Seven Demons, I marvel at how unconcerned they are over our presence. I admit, I've kind of gotten used to beings fearing me. Even the most powerful show some hint of fear under their bravado. Not the Demons. They are fully aware of the fact that taking out just one of them is a strain on my power. And even then, I can't actually kill one of them. Just capture it or remove it from my presence. With the help of my Familiars, of course. Who are standing by ready to fight when needed. Clearing my slowly constricting throat, I force my vocal cords to work again. "Before you is the only weapon of your mass destruction. The Angels did something to him to make him so. I haven't been able to figure out what. Given enough time, I would be able to, but I don't even want to contemplate how much destruction you would cause between now and then, how many lives would be lost. So, I offer you this. He is yours to do with as you will if you agree to leave the rest of the beings in all universes alone."

"All universes," one of the Demon scoffs. "You cannot bargain for all universes. Only your own."

Its words tell me two things. One, they are willing to bargain. I suspect the Demons know more about Keelan and the prophecy than they are willing to let on. Two, I need to bargain for all universes because I am beginning to suspect that Keelan was only infused with Demon blood in this one. As much as I hate my doppelganger, I can't leave hers or any other universe out there to the clutches of the Demons. "Nope, all or nothing," I say.

"We haff the child. We need not bargain wiff you," lispy Demon says. I look closer at him. I guess it would be harder to speak with no lips and only half a tongue. I know it only has half a tongue because it is also missing most of its teeth so I have a clear view into its mouth. Gross.

An idea had been growing in my mind since first hearing the prophecy. "If you could just snatch him, you would have done so already. No, you need him to be given freely. Otherwise, his power remains intact."

At least now we know which one roared earlier. It is difficult, but I refrain from covering my ears as the low rumbling threatens to shatter my eardrums. Okay, it's not that difficult. Lifting my arms that far would be an impossible feat. Alita's mother is back to holding me upright.

The roaring is cut off abruptly. My eyes cut to the Demon in the corner that is currently picking glass out of its skull. One of the other Demons smashed its cocktail glass against its head. I decide to the rattle the Demons a bit more. "That's what the whole changing reality thing was all about. You were trying to keep me busy and were holding her husband hostage while you figured out a way to force Alita to give up her child."

"Aren't you a clever little mutt?" one of the Demons growls. Turning its eyes, which are missing eyelids, to Alita, it demands, "Hand over the child."

I respond for her. "You haven't agreed to the terms yet," I remind it.

One of the other Demons pushes forward. Literally. It knocks one of its comrades over a steel and glass coffee table. The glass shatters. I wonder how often they need to redecorate this place. "What of you? Why have you not demanded to be cured?" Suspicion rings clear in its voice. "What trickery do you have planned?"

I give it a half-hearted shrug. I'm not capable of more at the moment. "I'm not stupid enough to believe that you would willingly return me to full power."

"What of your Angel friends? You do not demand to know what has been done to them?"

"Well, I did say you needed to leave all *beings* in all universes alone. The Angels are part of the universe." Technically. "Besides," I hurry to add, "You are already breaking your truce with the Angels simply by holding them captive. I seriously doubt you are risking an all-out war again by harming them." I hope. I really, really hope this is true.

"I do not trust her," the Demon declares. Several others concur.

I snort as loudly as my rapidly approaching demise will allow. "I'm dying. What good would it do me to try to trick you?"

"You would save those you love," one of the Demons spits. Literally. I have Demon saliva on my cheek. The sucker's like ten feet away. If I wasn't disgusted I'd be impressed with its distance and accuracy.

"You're right. That's what I'm doing with the trade." My next words cut a deep chasm into Alita's heart. "I am trading one I don't yet love for those I do love."

"I love him," Alita says softly.

"So do I," her mother echoes with so much sharp steel in her voice I believe her words cut straight through my ear drums and into my brain.

I push my growing guilt down a deep as I can. "Do we have a deal?" I ask.

One Demon has been holding back just observing the scene playing out in front of it. It has actually been leaning against a fireplace mantel in what I believe is supposed to be a supermodel pose. Hard to pull off with black, wilting skin and a bevy of open, puss filled wounds. I give it credit for having the self-esteem to try, though. "We have a deal."

The other six whirl around to face the one who is obviously the leader of The Seven. Their voices are loud and angry as they protest. But, it's too late. The deal has been made.

"We accept, as well." This shuts them up. "Come get the baby so we can go. I want to say good bye to my husband before I die." My voice is growing weaker by the second. I'm surprised they can hear me way across the spacious room. They really do have great hearing.

"It is done," the leader of The Seven declares. It strides forward on sure feet. Pretty good considering one of its feet is missing every other toe, starting with the big one. I would definitely need a cane if my foot was like that.

Stopping before Alita, the Demon holds out its hands. "Give me the child."

While the Demons were arguing, I made sure Alita, her mother and I were all holding hands. So, it is with one arm Alita must hand over her child. The Demon reaches out to take him.

Grandma was right. What gullible fools these Demons are.

32 CHAPTER

As soon as the Demon touches Keelan, the feathers I shoved into his blanket flare. The Demon, realizing it has been tricked, attempts to let go. Too late. It is trapped. The others try to rush forward, but they cannot move. They have been bound.

One of the hardest things I have ever done was hurt Keelan. When I placed the feathers in his blanket several minutes ago, I had to nick him with the sharp end of one of the quills. For his blood needed to mix with the blood on the feathers to make this work. Alita had tears in her eyes when she saw what I was doing, but there was trust there, as well despite our harsh words to one another. She nodded in encouragement when my hand faltered. It was what I needed to be able to complete my task. Now, the recipe for the Demon trap is complete.

The only ingredient missing to end this war once and for all is my magic.

I hope I'm strong enough for this. Gathering my remaining strength, I say the words to the spell that has been forming in my mind since I first figured out Grandma's rambling speech was actually a set of instructions. *"From the fires of hell these creatures were born, from the Flames of Truth their countenances torn. Spurned by hatred of what they can never be, battered and blinded by their own zealotry, let this traitorous blood given freely by one of their own, with our offerings topple them all from their fiery throne. Blood of the first, middle and last races, sullied and pure tokens of grace, within innocence all encased. Tainted not by history nor lore, no allegiance has the babe previously sworn. Draw within him the power of The Seven, a conduit to fuel the soldiers of heaven."*

"No!" The Demons finally understand what I have done. And it's too late for them to do anything about it.

Around us, Angels begin to appear. They have waited in the shadows ready to answer my call to the fight. They are glorious. Geared up for battle, their wings in their full glory, they have come to rid the universes once and for all of the threat of the Demon scourge.

"How?" the leader of The Seven rasps.

Half of my mouth slides up into a grin. The only half currently functioning properly. "Silly Demon, Keelan was never mine to give. Only his mother could give him to you and she never actually let go of him. Did you once hear her say the words 'take my son, he's yours?' or feel her grip on him lessen at all?" I will take the Demon's roar of displeasure to mean it did not hear her utter those words or feel anything remotely like that. Of course Alita would never give up her child to these creatures. She and I both knew that from the very beginning despite the talk of destinies. What mother would? "I only needed you to touch him while his mother and grandmother were touching him. Their fierce love and protectiveness along with my magic and the blood soaked feathers were always going to be your downfall."

"How did you know it was the blood of a traitor?" the Demon demands, wanting a complete accounting for the ultimate defeat.

I shrug. "That was a guess. I couldn't imagine most of you guys would willingly give up your blood, and if blood from battle would do the trick, the Angels would have won a long time ago." It seems one of the Demon masses was not as willing as the rest to let The Seven leach off it.

"Enough talk," an Angel I am not familiar with declares. All of the Angels and Demons immediately give him their attention.

I cock an eyebrow at Grandma who has appeared beside me. She whispers out of the corner of her mouth, "Gadriel, the Angel of War." I nod in understanding.

Not being able to keep my mouth shut, even when I'm dying, I ask Gadriel, "What are you going to do with them?"

Obsidian eyes turn my way. Quite the contrast to his white blond hair. Freaky. "This matter no longer concerns you."

Turns out I'm not too sick to snort. Eew, was that blood I just snorted out? "You know nothing about me if that is what you believe. I got you to this point. Without me," recognizing I was not alone in this, I add, "or Alita, her mother or Keelan and many others whom I love, you would not be standing here ready to swoop down and do your worst. So, this very much concerns me. And if you think that glare of yours is going to frighten me, remember, I just faced and trapped The Seven. Something you couldn't do. A glare really doesn't faze me at this point." Did Grandma just giggle next to me? I turn to look but her face is a serene mask.

"She is correct, Gadriel," a familiar voice says.

A door opens and another unfamiliar Angel leads Raziel and Adriel into the room. They were apparently being held in there. I scan them both for injury, but as I suspected, they are unharmed. Tired and probably hungry and thirsty, but not injured. The Seven were not about to risk all-out war by harming them. They just wanted them out of the way so Raziel would not tell us their plan. Too bad for them they didn't know about the prophecy. Raziel didn't need to be present to tell us all about it. It pays to be an omniscient Angel with forethought.

Raziel continues. "As impressive is your cunning and valor, it was Xandra who won this war. Her question is fair and deserving of a response."

Eyes as frosty as the hair on his head, Gadriel once again turns to me. "They will be slaughtered." Concise and to the point. Angel of few words, obviously.

"No." Did that word just come out of my mouth? I almost look around to see if maybe someone else is speaking, but it slowly dawns on me that I did say it. In fact, I have more to say. "They are powerless against you or anyone else now. Make sure they stay that way, but I did not sign on for genocide. If they are no longer a threat, then leave them be." Who knows. Maybe Demons can be rehabilitated. Seems doubtful, but shouldn't they at least be given the chance? Maybe not The Seven, but the ones in the pit might not be as bad as these guys.

"You dare give me orders?!" Gadriel roars. His vocals are not quite as impressive as the Demon's were, but he's pretty close.

"Yes." This time, there is a definite giggle coming from between Grandma's lips. She quickly stifles it when Gadriel glowers at her.

"No."

"I could give them their power back and let you fight them on your own," I half-heartedly threaten.

It's enough to whole-heartedly piss Gadriel off. "You threaten treason," he growls taking several menacing steps toward me.

"No, I am merely suggesting you fight your own battles if you're not going to listen to my input. After all, I did all the heavy lifting here."

Gadriel takes another step toward me and I am suddenly flanked by most of the Angels in the room. Their wings are outstretched and I get more than one feather in my mouth and nose. I try hard not to sneeze. It would ruin the effect.

Grandma and Raziel are at my side, each taking one of my hands. Adriel, Rashnu, Urim, Tabbris, Ray and all the other Angels I know by name and many that I don't are also ready to stand with me against this Angel of War. My heart would swell with pride if it wasn't being constricted by Demon poison.

Gadriel stops and takes in the sight before him. The black orbs on either side of his nose narrow as he stares at each Angel in turn. I see the instant he realizes he is beaten. It's in the subtle slumping of his shoulders, an almost indiscernible movement. "Our fallen brethren deserve better than this." He is not talking about Fallen Angels. He is talking of those who lost their lives in battle.

"They were fighting to rid the universes of the evil perpetrated by the Demons. That has been accomplished," Raziel reminds him. "It is not our place to pass ultimate judgement."

This argument is already won. Everyone here knows it. So, I feel perfectly comfortable saying to those closest to me, "Can I go home now? I would really like to die with Kallen by my side."

Grandma pulls me into a hug. "Darling, how you must be suffering." I feel her motioning to someone behind my back. Suddenly, Alita and Keelan are next to me. They had been politely shoved behind the Angels who came to protect me a moment ago. Letting me go, Grandma instructs, "Hold the babe."

Um, as much as I would like to hold Keelan one more time, I'm not really strong enough. "I'd drop him," I admit.

Alita comes closer. "We will hold him together," she says softly. I stare at her in wonder. There is no animosity in her eyes, no hatred. I used her child as a tool in a war with Demons and she somehow has forgiven me already. Seeing the awe in my eyes, she says, "It was his destiny, and I am proud that my son helped you accomplish this great feat."

Oh, okay then. I extend my arms and wrap them around Keelan. Alita moves closer so I don't need to support all of his weight as I pull him close. To my great surprise, he begins to glow again like he did in the tunnels when he was guiding us. Only this time, the glow extends until it is surrounding both Alita and me.

As pretty of a picture as we probably make surrounded by this blue light, the removal of poison is never a painless process. Just like when my wings cleansed me of poison in the past, Keelan's light cleansing me is painful as hell. The poison that was removed from my system before was nothing compared to Demon poison. This poison has apparently found every single blood cell in my body and it is clinging to them with extended claws as Keelan's magic tries to yank it off each and every one. It rips completely through more than one blood cell. I'm pretty sure I'm bleeding internally, but I can't heal that until all the poison is gone. I just hope I have the strength for it by the time Keelan is done. Or, technically, the Demon magic currently coursing through him. I do my best not to cry out, not wanting to the scare the child. I do shake and tremble with pain. There is sympathy in the eyes of those around me, but no one can do anything to stop it. It is either remove the poison or I die.

I thought walking through the Demon labyrinth took a long time. That was nothing compared to how long it takes to remove Demon poison. By the time Keelan is finished, I am lying prone on the ground, Alita next to me making sure I am still cradling her son so the magic doesn't stop. From the ornate clock over the mantel, I know that an hour has passed. Whether or not a clock in the Demon labyrinth tells accurate time, I do not know.

When it is done, the blue light bathing us begins to dim. Alita is helped to her feet with Keelan still in her arms. I hear voices around me and I know the Angels have borrowed Keelan from Alita. The power of The Seven must be removed from his system before it destroys him. The last thing I hear before I lose the battle of consciousness to the internal bleeding is Alita's quiet sobbing as she hands her son over for what may be a painful procedure of his own. I really, really hope it's not.

33 Chapter

My eyes flutter open and my favorite voice in any reality says, "If you want us to live a long and happy life together, you really should stop shaving years off my mortality by returning to me on the brink of death so often." The chastisement is not spoken all in jest.

I reach a hand up and cup his cheek, marveling at the fact that I have the strength to do it. And that I can do it pain-free. "As I do every time, I apologize and promise to try to make it up to you."

A sexy grin forms on Kallen's lips. "I already have a list in mind."

"I'm sure you do," I purr.

"Perhaps this is a conversation better suited for somewhere other than the living room," Isla drawls.

My eyes dart around the room and I realize she is right. Not only are we in the living room, we are surrounded by everyone we care about. It seems my blood levels have been restored, because there is plenty of it inside me to rush to my face without my legs feeling numb. "Sorry," I mumble.

Kallen chuckles and helps me to a sitting position. Not easy considering the fact that I still have my wings. They must have been healing me while I was unconscious. I have never loved my wings more than I do at this moment. Scanning the room again, my eyes rest on Alita and Kegan. Keelan is cradled in his father's arms and I blurt out to the new parents, "I'm sorry I had to use Keelan as a weapon." To Alita specifically, I say, "I'm especially sorry for the things I said down there. I didn't mean any of them."

Alita nods. "You couldn't let the Demons in on your plans, I know." There is still a lingering tinge of hurt in her eyes, but I know in her heart she really has forgiven me.

A thought slams into my brain. "Oh my god, Tana!" I exclaim. I passed out before I could make the Demon relinquish its hold on Tana.

"Here," a soft voice says from across the room. My eyes fly to her and I find my step-mother molded against my father's side. I doubt he's going to be letting her go for a very long time. That might get awkward in some of his meetings as King, but I'm sure he'll make it work.

I am relieved to see that her eyes have returned to a pleasant shade of green versus silver or red. The Demon is definitely gone. "I'm sorry we couldn't save you sooner," I say lamely.

Kallen puts a hand on my chin and turns my head toward him. "Will you please stop apologizing? You just saved the universe from Demons, a feat the Angels themselves could not accomplish. Trust me when I say all is forgiven."

Raziel grins down at me from over the back of the couch I am currently sitting on. "Take it from someone who can see the future. No one is holding a grudge over anything that happened today."

I narrow my eyes at him. "Are you supposed to tell me things like that?"

With a wink, he says, "I have been given special leeway in this particular situation."

"So we discovered. Thanks for that prophecy, by the way. And yes, I did feel morally desolate," I grumble. "What about Grandma. Was she given permission to tell me the things she did?"

Raziel nods. "She rehearsed that speech many times, for it had to sound like the ramblings of a worried grandmother instead of a recipe for a spell."

"She did a great job. If she hadn't slipped me that feather, I never would have figured it out. I have another question. Why could Alita and her mother see the Angels? And you and Adriel for that matter." Fallen Angels can't see their counterparts without reacting like mere mortals in their presence. Blindness, death, etc.

"The rules are different in the Demon labyrinth," Raziel explains. "The veils are lifted for there can be nothing but truth there." I'm not sure exactly what that means, but I'll take his word for it.

My eyes are drawn to Keelan again. "Will he be okay?"

Alita nods. "The Angels assured me he would. It did not even hurt when they drew the Demon magic from him."

I bite my bottom lip trying not to ask the next question. Kegan answers it anyway. "He still retains magic. We do not know how strong he will be since all traces of Demon magic were stripped from him, but likely as strong as I am at the very least." Kegan smiles like the proud father he is.

I smile in return. "I'm glad to hear that." Now, for the question which will determine how eager I am to work with the Angels in the future. Directing my question to Raziel and Adriel, who is standing next him, I brace myself for the answer. "What did the Angels do with the Demons?"

Adriel's lips curl into an evil little smile. "Nothing."

"What?"

"Absolutely nothing. They were left in their labyrinth."

"Technically, they were left in the pit," Raziel corrects. "The Seven get to spend eternity with the rest of their kind languishing in the pit with no hope of a better existence."

"That may actually be a punishment worse than death," I muse.

"My parents have returned home, but my mother did have a request before she left," Alita tells me with a mischievous smile. "The next time you decide to travel to hell, she would like you to leave without her."

I laugh. "I will keep that in mind." Sobering, I explain, "I had to take her, though. Keelan needed to be surrounded by those who love him deeply to keep him comfortable and feeling safe in order for him to guide us, and you needed the support, as well. Kegan was out of the question. He would have done something rash and stupid and the Demons would have seen him as a threat and killed him immediately."

My husband chuckles beside me. "She knows you so well, Cousin," he tells a glowering Kegan.

"Actually, it was Grandma's idea," I admit. "Keelan also drew strength from the familial bond when we stood united as I spoke the spell."

Kegan's nose wrinkles. "He may have just saved the universe, but his diaper is about to destroy the inside of my nostrils. I will take him upstairs to the nursery and change him." Fatherhood has definitely changed him. He didn't even rise to the bait of my and Kallen's teasing other than his glower. Impressive.

"After several days in hell, I could really use a shower," Adriel announces.

There is distinct lust in Raziel's eyes as he says, "I could, as well." It's not hard to figure out that they will not be showering alone.

"I would like to return home and rest," Tana tells Dagda.

Dagda smiles indulgently. "Of course, anything you want." Though, from the lust in both of their eyes, I don't think they will be doing a whole lot of resting. Eew. At least they seem to have forgotten about the episode between Mom and Dagda. Speaking of which, I search the room for my parents. I am relieved to find them across the room standing together. Dad has a casual arm slung around Mom's waist and they are smiling. All seems to be well with them, too.

Kallen stands up and says with a wink, "You look like you could use some rest, as well."

Now, the lust in his eyes is far from eew. "Most definitely." I don't even bother to say good bye to anyone before teleporting us to our room. They must be used to that by now.

In our bedroom, Kallen removes our clothes and leads me to the shower. My wings are about to get very wet. Which is okay since I was lying on the ground in the Demon labyrinth. I'm sure they could use a good washing.

Standing under the perfect temperature spray, I kiss my perfect husband. "I thought I was going to die," I murmur against his lips. For once, I honestly thought I was going to die. After all, the Angels have no cure for Demon poisoning.

Kallen smiles against my lips. "Good thing I had faith enough for both of us that you would not. You see, you are not allowed to die without me."

I quirk an eye brow. "I'm not?"

He shakes his head. "You are not. The love we share is too great. You are bound to me for eternity and nothing can get in the way of that. Not even death. Though, I would appreciate it if you would stop testing that theory."

Smiling against his lips, I purr, "I will do my best. If you could ask the universe to do the same, I would greatly appreciate it."

"I have already put in my request to the powers that be."

The time for words is done. I press my lips against Kallen's and we spend the next several hours proving to the universe that its threats of tearing us apart do not scare us. We will survive anything it throws at us and will celebrate our victories in each other's arms every single time.

Printed in Great Britain
by Amazon